Other books by John D. Carter

Intelligence and Attention

Intimacy in Cocktail Lounges

Belle Islet Lady

Crazy Cousins

To Amrit
Have a great summer!
All good wishes
and smiles
John

CAPE LAZO

a Novel

BY

JOHN D. CARTER

Cover photography:
Hugo Chisholm cc 2015, via Flickr.com
Used under Creative Commons License v4.0.

Cover and Book Design: Vladimir Verano, Third Place Press

Published by

John D. Carter

Belle.Islet@gmail.com

Second Printing

ISBN: 978-0-9940346-2-5

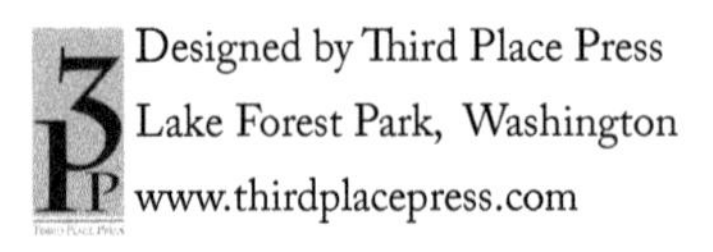

There is a Cape Lazo on Vancouver Island.

The Comox Valley, Forbidden Plateau, and Desolation Sound are all described in this book. They are real, but the majority of the rest is fiction. All the events and the characters are products of my imagination. Most of the geographical, historical, and nautical descriptions are fairly accurate. Nonetheless, some literary liberties are taken here and there in this depiction of Cape Lazo.

It is not what you look at that matters, it is what you see.

~Henry David Thoreau

Life is what happens while you are busy making other plans.

~John Lennon – *Beautiful Boy*

TABLE OF CONTENTS

PART ONE

I. Packing Problems 1
II. Forbidden Plateau 7
III. Cape Lazo 15
IV. Mr. Maxwell's Friend 25
V. Orcinus Orca 30
VI. Perfect Presents 39
VII. Cinderella's Sister 48
VIII. Mount Mania 58
IX. Desolation Sound 65
X. Squirrel Cover 74
XI. Going Home 80
XII. Epilogue: Seven Years Later 83

PART TWO

I. Socratic Symptoms 91
II. Annie Jarman 101
III. Parisian Prebendaries 105
IV. Letters to Annie 111
V. Pygmy Dreams 116
VI. Whistler Mountain 122
VII. Victor Hugo Boulevard 126
VIII. Cranial Chemistry 138
IX. Schizophrenia's Rule of Quarters 141
X. Which Wolfe Was It? 144
XI. Gentle Genetics 148
XII. Penultimate Possibilities and a Puppy 151
XIII. Cape Lazo Redux 154

Acknowledgements 159

PART ONE

I.

PACKING PROBLEMS

When I first heard we were moving to Vancouver Island, I about near died, certainly cried. I mean really, leaving Montreal was the absolute last thing in the world I'd want to do. I love Montreal. All my friends live in Montreal. Fort Ville-Marie is where I want to be. Nurdos live elsewhere. There is nowhere else worthwhile to live. Okay, the world is not flat, but Montreal is where it is at, and I just do not want to move. Why would I want to move?

My dad, yes that is who wants to move clear across to the other side of the country. Trouble is I can't argue with him. Well, I can't argue like I might normally. My dad likes arguing. He is really good at arguing. He does it for a living. People pay him money to argue for them. Yes sir, a professional person to argue on your behalf: My father. These days, he is under doctors' orders not to argue with anyone for any reason. That means me too. Stress, he is not supposed to have any for a while. You see he's still recovering from a recent heart attack. Literally, he about near died. Dad had the ticking time bomb syndrome or something like that is what the doctors called it.

He is only fifty-two years old! "Way too young for his number to be called," at least that's what Mr. Maxwell, one of the senior partners at *Dinning, Maxwell, and Myers*, the law firm where my dad worked, said while we were in the hospital's waiting room.

It was weird; I mean really weird. When they finally let me see dad he looked terrible. He had all these tubes with clamps, and crappy looking loud machines wired up to him. Like the thing was that I was standing there talking to him and I don't think he knew what was going on. He just lay there looking at me. His eyes were open, but it was a blank stare. It was weird.

When Mr. Maxwell came to Sir Wilfred Laurier Middle School to take me to the hospital, I got to leave math early. No one, I mean not even the Vice Principal, Mr. Metzger, would dare argue with Mr. Alan K. Maxwell, Queens Counsel QC, OBE, PQ. I felt so weird walking down that long school hallway. Mr. Maxwell wears loud shoes – BIG black brogues. I felt like this thing with dad was my fault. I felt so bad about all the fighting, bickering, and bull tweed. We had been arguing quite a bit lately. My schoolwork, video games, and late night television programmes were some of the starters. But, geez, when we got going, we could argue about anything. One time I was so picked with my dad I found myself arguing that only dorks wore socks to school. Now all I could think of was, oh God, Buddha, whoever or whatever you are, give us another chance. Please!

Truth was my dad's heart attack wasn't really all my fault. I felt a bit better knowing that. And I felt a lot better knowing he wasn't going to die. According to Dr. Leonard, and Mr. Maxwell, dad had been working way, way too hard. He was under too much stress, he'd been taking on too many things and it all just caved in on him. Even still, I knew, deep down inside, I could have made things easier for him at home. I don't know why we would argue over stupid things. We just did. It was the way we were, the way we played this father/son game.

Dad was, until the heart-thing, a real big time corporate lawyer in one of the largest and most prestigious law firms in Montreal. And I guess maybe that's why he was always working all the time. I mean he worked all the time. He would start working before breakfast, during breakfast, and then way on into the middle of the night. I think he liked taking on tough stuff. He liked to be challenged. Weird, eh, the working thing, what's the deal with that?

Some Sundays we would go down to his office. When I was a little kid, going to dad's office was just one of the best things you could do on a Sunday. His office was awesome. His secretary had her desk outside dad's office. She hardly never ever came in on Sundays; so I got to goof around with all her stuff, like the computer, copy machine, dictation machines, and phone headset. What I really loved best, when I was a little kid, was spinning down the hall on her office chair.

The view from dad's window was outstandingly excellent. The office was on the thirty-fourth floor. Actually, the law firm was so big that they needed five floors to hold all the lawyers, secretaries, and legal-type people who walked around the place like they knew what they were doing. Dad had a corner office on the top floor. You knew he was important because he had such a big office.

Sunday was the best day to visit the office because there were never many people around and I could have the run of the place. Some Sundays Mr. Maxwell would be working. He's cool. He'd always invite me into his office, tell me to sit down, "take a load off," and have a Pepsi. Mr. Maxwell was the kind of man who was definitely a good listener. It seemed like he really wanted to hear what I thought about things. And what's more, he had a way of making me feel like I could talk to him about anything and everything. He was one guy I could count on to listen and make me feel like it was an important worthwhile discussion. I mattered. He didn't judge me.

Mr. Maxwell had the whitest hair I'd ever seen. He said that's why the other lawyers called him the silver fox. Dad said they called him the silver fox because he was sly and awfully clever. I knew he was clever, but I'd never think of him as sly. Smart sounds better than sly.

I loved to hear Mr. Maxwell's stories about when he was a kid growing-up in Newfoundland. His family lived in a fishing community where his father fished for cod off the Grand Banks. Mr. Maxwell made Atlantic Ocean fishing sound so exciting. Dad was always saying we'd go fishing sometime. But, sometimes *sometime* doesn't quite get-it-together to happen when I want it to or thought it should. "We will do it *sometime.*"

My most favourite story was about the time when Mr. Maxwell's big black Newfoundland dog saved a man who had been washed overboard from a trawler by a series of huge waves. "The Atlantic was mean and cold," Mr. Maxwell said, shaking his finger at me, "Sure death lurks for anyone in that water for any length of time."

The captain and crew tried throwing ropes to the man, but it was no use. Finally, in desperation, Mr. Maxwell's father tied a rope around the big Newfie dog's neck. He had to be careful how he tied the rope. It had to be tight enough to hold the man as well as the seventy-kilogram dog.

The dog leaped into the freezing water and you could only see him for a few seconds and then a wave would hit and then there would be no sign of him at all. But, after what seemed like an eternity amount of time the big dog reached the floundering man. The man was so close to death he could hardly hang on to the rope. He kept slipping under the surface and the dog would pull him back up to the surface by the scruff of his neck.

The men on the boat pulled and strained on the rope like madmen. Then, when the dog was only about six metres off the stern, a mountainous rogue wave came crashing over the boat. After the men recovered from the impact, the rope was gone. Everyone gave up hope. That is, until deep from within the blackened freezing water came a loud bellowing roar. The big Newfoundland dog had made it back.

The man, half dead from hypothermia, was still clutching a piece of rope. They almost had to break his fingers in order to get the unconscious fisherman to release his grip. The big dog was everyone's hero.

Once I asked Mr. Maxwell why he ever became a lawyer in the first place. He said it was what his father wanted.

"Didn't he want you to be a fisherman?" I asked.

Mr. Maxwell gazed down at his desk. "My father thought that he wanted me to become something more important than an ordinary Newfoundland fisherman," Mr. Maxwell replied. "My father didn't want me risking my life on a rickety fish boat, day in day out, in the worst of weathers. He wanted me to be all that he couldn't. But, little did he know how important he was to me," he added solemnly. "When father died there were so many things I wish I could have told him when he was alive," he said sliding the photograph to me.

In a way, looking at the photograph, I could see how similar they were, but different too. It wasn't just their clothing either. I don't know how to say it, except it was in their faces. Mr. Maxwell's dad looked like he belonged there, sitting beside his boat fixing a net. I certainly can't say the same for Mr. Maxwell, QC, OBE, PQ. I picture him better out on the open sea with the wind whistling threw his curly gray hair. Somehow Mr. Maxwell didn't look quite right sitting behind a big oak desk, at the top of a glass and concrete tower.

Moving sucks. I mean it was just way too stupid to believe that this was really happening. I was told to pack my "personal effects" and the movers would do the rest. Like it is as if I would trust movers to pack my prized possessions. I didn't want to move! I'd miss Mr. Maxwell, my friends, and all the kewl places we'd go to.

We moved once before. I can't remember very much about it because I was only five years old. Back then, my mum and dad were still married – to each other. We lived in a nice little house out in the country with a big back yard. Dad commuted to Montreal. He said they broke up because of his work. Truth was mum had an affair with one of dad's friends. That's what did it, but you'd never know from dad. The only way I found out was years later when I read his old journal diary that he filled up, put it on the top selves of the big bookshelf, and started a new one. He has a dozens of journal diaries. He writes everyday, and then when one is full, he starts another just like it. A bedtime ritual that described what he did every day.

Mum moved to New York. First she lived in Greenwich Village, and then she married a rich guy named Anthony, and moved to Long Island. She divorced Anthony and now she's married to a playwright named Donald. They live in a fancy, high-security apartment in Manhattan. I visit them three times a year for a real long weekends and then two weeks in the summer. Donald's basically okay, but his daughter from a previous marriage also comes to visit the same time as I do. Mum and Donald like to take care of visitations in a package deal.

I really hate Donald's daughter. They call her Ronnie (short for Veronica). You can imagine what I call her. She just drives me completely crazy!

"Ronnie is from California," chirped my mother. "Ronnie goes to a very exclusive prep school where a number of famous movie stars' children also attend."

Ronnie this, Ronnie that. I could barf. I mean really; it just drove me completely nuts. It's nice to know someone who is perfect but even extreme perfection gets a little bit boring after a while.

Boring, boring, boring and then a bit more boring on the side. I knew Vancouver Island would be boring. For one thing, nobody lives there. I mean there are more people living on my block in Montreal than there are people in the town we are moving to. I think there are more people living in our apartment building than in the place we are going. This moving thing is a very BIG mistake, but you think dad would listen to me. No chance at all, the move was happening, according to dad, "Whether I liked it or not. The move was happening. Get on board we are moving westward ho."

"Oh no," I said to myself and anyone else who would listen.

Dad suggested I call the Children's Help Line, but he expected they would likely hang up on me on this issue.

II.

FORBIDDEN PLATEAU

You would never know what a large country Canada really is until you have to drive across from one end to the other. It took us six days. Dad likes to stop and look at things. He likes to stop for coffee, lunch, afternoon coffee, and all assorted "points of interest." He photographed the entire trip start to finish. Why we would not fly was my question. He simply replied that he wanted to "enjoy the scenery."

We stopped in Winterpeg for a week one afternoon. Get it. We had to visit my Uncle Jody and Aunt Sue. All I can report is: Big-time Boring. That is, except for Aunt Sue's cookies and Uncle Jody's DVD movie collection and satellite dishes, telescope, and drones. Their television gets something like a zillion different stations. Like it's not as though I got to count because I finally found a channel I liked and we were called to dinner.

The next day we left early for the flatlands. No lie, really, I thought he said "Vagina" was the biggest city in Saskatchewan. Turns out the name of the city is Regina – like the queen I guess. I dunno, in my social studies class we study Quebec. Definitely not my fault, dad.

Actually, the flatlands were not quite as flat as I had thought they were supposed to be, and there were some semi-scenic parts, too. Dad went on at great length how the Great Plains First Nations Indians lived off the land in tee-pees. Buffalo were well suited to the plains, but the white men killed as many as they could. Almost driving the buffalo into extinction. Replaced with dumb dull domesticated cows. That was the white man's way. And they had the audacity to call it progress. Mad cow disease did not come from Buffalo.

After clearing the flatlands we stopped in the Rocky Mountain town called Banff and later stayed the night at Chateau Lake Louise. I loved the old Chateau and the emerald coloured lake. Dad explained that originally the only way into the Chateau was by Canadian Pacific Railway. It wasn't until years later that road access was blasted through the mountain. They wanted a road rather than rail.

The Chateau's restaurant was wonderful, too. The grand old Canadian tradition of French fries and gravy was just as good as our old neighbourhood's finest eatery that served the very best poutine and beaver tail desserts. However, I could not tell dad that because I was still awfully resentful and angry about moving to the other side of the planet. Why would we leave Montreal?

The next morning we were up way way too early. Dad, ever the adventurer, decided to get off the main route and take the Crows Nest Pass. I do not know how to drive. Do not hold a license and therefore not allowed to criticize, but oh geez dad you are going to get us killed in the Rockies. The road was weird and wound around rocks at steep angles. For a living, dad drives courtrooms. He jostles judges and cajoles juries. In Montreal he takes a taxi everywhere (Mr. Maxwell explains that someone of dad's stature cannot afford to ever, never drink and drive). Dad does not drive cars very much and I just did not think he was doing an adequate good job driving through the Rockies. He, on the other hand, was having a most excellent time. He thought this was superb scenery and enjoyed the BMW's cornering and magnificent maneuvering. I thought we would die. This moving this was a dumb idea. A really dumb idea.

After *six* days the next thing I knew we were on a giant ferry going across the Georgia Strait and Salish Sea to Vancouver Island. The ferry was like a huge multilevel moving parking lot travelling in the ocean. Dad said the ferry docked in Nanaimo and then it was *only* a short one hundred and fifty-five kilometers to the Comox Peninsula, our new home.

You can hardly imagine my excitement. It wasn't too hard to keep a lid on it, but I exercised tolerance. Mostly, it was because dad was really, really up for this whole thing. He was uber excited and it was good for him. I hadn't seen him this happy since the book he published on "Debentures in Canada" won an award. So you see, how could I spoil it all by telling him that this Vancouver Island business was doomed for gloom? We should have stayed in Montreal.

Prior to actually leaving on "the big trip," dad and I had sort of a mini-fight over the whole thing. Dad's temper boiled over and he threatened to make me go live in Manhattan with my mum and Donald. And of course, just to hold up my end of the fight, I said, "Yeah, well Manhattan would be one heck of a lot better than this hair-brained idea of moving clear across the country to some deserted Island." Naturally, right after I said it I felt like a piece of poop. I knew he wasn't trying to do this to me on purpose. He thought – I mean he said it enough times – this move would be good for the two of us.

So, for him, I agreed to give it a try. It was the least I could do for dad. And, as he coaxingly asked, "You wouldn't want me to live there all by myself?"

Now, the "Island Highway" is another story in and of itself. I mean it's a lie. You can't call a narrow, twisty, turning, not-quite-even-two-lanes in places, a highway. In Montreal, they'd laugh you clear out of your BMW for calling that wobbly line of asphalt a highway.

Dad had been telling me that the pace of life was much slower on the Island than what we were used to in Montreal. It's called Island-time. "Yeah dad, I'm sure that is why they drive a million kilometers an hour and ride on our rear bumper flashing their headlights to pass. I mean these guys get so close to our back seat that I can read the name of the tire company that sold 'em their baseball cap. And they all wear baseball caps.

We had driven across the whole country. I wasn't really all that extremely nervous going through the Rocky Mountains. I was only moderately nervous crawling through the Fraser Canyon. But this "Island Highway" was something else. I mean my normally curly hair was straightening out when dad didn't slow down enough for the hairpin turn at Cougar Creek. We practically skidded out and landed in the ditch.

Research. Oh yes, dad is real big on research. All the way up the Island Highway he told me about what he had discovered researching the geographic and cultural history of our "new home."

"Peter, I bet you didn't know the Comox Valley (that's where we're moving to) was named by the Indians as "The Land of Plenty," he said, as a semi-trailer truck passed us as though we were standing still.

He went on to tell me why it was a valley. As if I didn't know what a dingledorfheaded valley was!

"The westerly part of the valley is bordered by the Beaufort Mountain Range that runs down the Island. The other side is bordered by the Georgia Strait, Salish Sea and the Garibaldi Mountains on the mainland," he continued.

I must admit that after a while some of the things he was talking about started to sound a little bit interesting. I mean anything was more interesting than sitting there wondering when we would crash or when someone was going to ram us from behind. I kept wondering what I did with the "Last Will and Testament of Peter Martin Mackintosh" that Bodhi Kuppers and I drafted last summer on a slow day.

"The Comox Indians lived in the valley because it had plenty of fish, wild game, and berries," he said.

One little tidbit of research dad dug up about the Comox Indians was the "Legend of the Forbidden Plateau."

"One day, and I'm not making this up, Peter," dad lamented as he began the story. "The Alberni Indians who lived to the south of the Comox tribe, came and attacked the unsuspecting, and heretofore, peaceful Comox Indians. The Alberni Indians were merciless. They killed all the Comox men they could catch at the camp and they kidnapped the younger women for slaves. They destroyed the Comox camp by setting it on fire."

Dad had my attention now. This was much more interesting than that political socio-economic stuff he was going on about before we got into the cultural history of the place.

"Not all of the Comox Indians were killed that day," dad continued. "There had been a deer hunting party out of camp as well as a number of men who had been fishing off the other side of the peninsula where they couldn't hear or see what was happening back at camp. There were also a number of women and children who had left the camp earlier that day to go pick some of the thousands of blackberries that were ripening in the sun. When all these remaining Comox Indians finally returned to camp, their grief was immeasurable. They couldn't believe what had happened."

Dad had my attention, "What happened next?"

Dad cleared his throat and continued, "One of the Comox men who the Albernis had left for dead was beginning to moan as he regained consciousness with hearing familiar voices returning to camp. His brother rushed towards him and held him in his arms. The dying man lived long enough to tell what had happened."

The Comox men were crazy with grief and anger. Some wanted to rush off after the Albernis and cut their heads off. However, the man whose brother had told the story of the Albernis sneak attack maintained a cooler, more calculating head. He had a plan. The Comox Indians would not be caught off guard next time. He knew the marauding Albernis would be back. This time, they'd be ready.

They gathered all the old men, women, and children together the next day. They were being sent away to hide up in the plateau that looked down upon the Comox camp. The old men protested, they wanted to fight. However, their protests fell on deaf ears. They were ordered to lead the women and children up to the plateau where they would remain until the war was over.

The Comox men were now warriors. Until now they had always been a peaceful people. Not now. They were driven with revenge.

They knew that when the Albernis returned they would have to go through the mountain pass at Tsable Mountain. Near where Poum Lake and the Tsable River meet, the Comox warriors waited. They had set many traps all along the area where the Albernis would pass through. One trap was made in such a way that when given the signal a Comox warrior would cut a piece of rawhide and an avalanche of rocks would pour down the hill on top of the Albernis.

This time the Albernis were going to get a dose of their own medicine. This time it was the Albernis who were not expecting an attack.

The Comox warriors waited patiently for a long time at their positions. Finally, the lookout scout sounded the bird's call to alert them that the Albernis were coming. The unsuspecting Albernis walked right into the trap, just as the Comox warriors had planned.

When all the Albernis had advanced far enough into the trap and there was no escape route left open to them, the signal was given. Boulders, logs, spears, and arrows poured upon the Albernis. When the dust settled enough to see, the Comox warriors flew from their positions to finish off any Alberni that still had life in him.

The Comox warriors had been victorious. They knew the Albernis would never bother them again. They spent the night celebrating the victory. Huge fires lit the entire sky while the warriors sang and danced to their victory. They danced and sang in honour of all the Comox people who had died before. For now, they could rest in peace. The score had been settled.

The next day they returned to their camp on the peninsula. A messenger was sent up the plateau to tell the old men, women, and children that it was safe to return.

Much, much later that day the messenger came running and screaming back to camp. He cried, "Our people have all disappeared. They are nowhere to be found! I searched everywhere all over the plateau and there is nobody there."

None of them could believe what they heard. It was getting close to sundown, nonetheless, a large search party set off to find their missing people.

It was no use. They searched every crook and cranny of the plateau and still there was no sign of what had happened, or where their people had gone. Cries of what were victory yesterday, turned into agony that night.

Finally, all they could conclude was evil spirits from within the plateau had taken their people. Further searching would be useless. The plateau was possessed. The men agreed from that day onward, a Comox Indian would never set foot on the plateau again. It was a Forbidden Plateau. And to this very day, you will never see a First Nations Indian set foot on that plateau."

My dad could spin one hell of a tale. "Dad, was that a true story?" I asked. "I mean, what happened to the Comox men? Did they become extinct? All their women were gone and that means: no women, no more babies."

"Yes Peter, you are partly correct," he said. "The Comox tribe would have become extinct when all their women had vanished. However, after their war with the Albernis, the Comox were strong and confident warriors. To ensure their tribe could continue the Comox warriors attacked another weaker tribe to the north. They stole their strongest and most beautiful women. That way, in time, they were able to rebuild their people."

When my dad said a story was true it always was. I told you; he's a lawyer, the kind that never lies. Even still, it was a hard story to swallow, especially when he – as Mr. Maxwell would say – threw the hook, line, and sinker at me.

"You know what else I uncovered in my research Peter?" he asked. "People have gone on record saying sometimes, in the late winter, when the sun and the moon are in a certain position, sections of snow on Forbidden Plateau turn a reddish colour, and nobody knows or can explain why it happens. But, there are those who say the snow turns red from the blood of the Comox Indians from long ago."

I sat there in the navigator's seat of our car just gawking out the window as the giant Douglas fir trees rolled by in a green sea of trunks and branches. I don't know but the whole time I could picture First Nations Indians camouflaged in between the trees watching us go by. Dog Soldiers.

I closed my eyes leaning my head back on the seat thinking about the snow turning red. I didn't doubt the veracity of dad's story but I thought the snow probably turned red due to iron or some sort of magnesium alloy in the dirt that somehow was reflected or refracted with the sunlight. But, on the other hand, I have a lot of respect for the First Nations Indians. Our social studies teacher, Mrs. Wagner (the coolest teacher in the whole stupid school), called 'em the aboriginal first peoples. She said their culture was very advanced, but the English, French, and Spanish came over in droves bringing an advanced form of bigotry and ethnocentrisms. The European's thought their culture was the best and they were going to save the First Nations Indians by teaching them their culture and taking away the aboriginal culture.

Glad I'm not ethnocentric…

III.

CAPE LAZO

"Peter," dad said somewhat softly but firm enough to rouse me, "Wake up we're almost there." He pointed up the road and said, "That's Cape Lazo, just up the road a little bit more."

Guess I must have nodded off. I missed turning off the highway, and now we were travelling along a funky little road beside the sea. The best thing about it was: We were the only people on the road. There was not another car in sight.

"Look over there Peter," dad said gesturing to the southeast, "See those two islands over there? If I'm not mistaken the one farthest to the left is Hornby and the other is Denman Island."

Dad had received a lot of information and stories from Mr. Johnston at the law firm. They had been pretty good friends. Dad said they had worked on some tough cases together. In fact, it's Mr. Johnston's house on Cape Lazo we were going to live.

Mr. Johnston's father built the house a long time ago in the other century. When Johnston Senior died, Junior Johnston inherited the house and everything that went with it. But dad says Junior Johnston never lived in the place since he graduated from UBC's Law School. Junior Johnston wanted to "hit the big time." So, he took a position and moved to Montreal. Dad had helped him get a toehold into the firm. After that, Mr. Johnston started his rise to the top. He works about as hard as dad once did, you know, before the heart-thing. Anyway, Mr. Johnston doesn't get back to Vancouver Island very often anymore and the Cape Lazo house just sits empty.

At first dad missed the turn-off. I mean they don't use signs or anything like that on these roads. You're just supposed to know where you're going. At any rate, we found the driveway hidden by some tall Douglas fir trees. As we made our way up the driveway, the house came into view. It was a big old house that looked simply majestic perched in a clearing overlooking the ocean.

Built within a stone's throw to the water, the house had an outrageously excellent view of the beach, Georgia Strait, and the mountains way across the water on the mainland. All around the house stood huge Douglas fir and Red Cedar trees. The beach was literally littered with washed-up pieces of driftwood.

Over to the side of the walkway to the beach was the boathouse. I raced down to take a look, and although the windows were pretty dirty, inside I could see what appeared to be a sailboat. "Yo dad," I yelled, "Come on down here and bring those keys."

It was no use. Dad was already making his way inside the house. I have long since learned that it is harder to turn him around once he has started than it is to join him. So I ran up to the house to tell him of my discovery.

Dad was opening the curtains to the big window that looked out over the water when I came in.

"Dad there's a sailboat in that boathouse down there," I said pointing to the beach. "Can we use it?"

"Of course Peter, Andy Johnston also said that there are a couple of canoes in the boathouse that you can use," dad replied. "First though, let's get settled a bit and then we'll go exploring. Here, help me with these suitcases, and you better pick a room before I get it."

Picking a bedroom was no trouble. I took the upstairs corner-room that had two windows, which meet at the corner. Excellent view. I could look all down the beach, across the water, and to the side where the huge towering evergreens stood.

My bed was called a roughhewn captain's bed. That means, as dad explained to me, the bed was made from cedar wood that hadn't been made smooth by a machine. Whatever way you look at it, the bed was indeed very, very, comfortable. It had three drawers underneath for clothes and stuff. The shelves along the paneled wainscoted walls were also made from cedar like the bed. They were perfecto for putting my prized possessions on. The bedroom was actually quite okay I kind of liked it. Even though we were in the middle of nowhere.

I started exploring and found that the rest of the house was pretty interesting, too. Dad's bedroom was down the hall from mine. He picked it because it had a big bay window with an old desk tucked next to it. There were three more bedrooms for visitors. But, as I said to dad, "Who'd ever visit us in this part of the world?"

Depending on the time of day, your attention on the main floor was either drawn to the big wooden table off the kitchen – especially if you're hungry for one of dad's famous flapjack and bacon breakfasts. Or, if the sun's shining, on a clear day – but even on a rainy day, you couldn't help but stare out the big picture window in the middle of the main floor. Or, then again, if it was nighttime, a person could snuggle-up on the big leather couch in front of the massive fireplace. The fireplace was made from river rocks. Mr. Johnston's father had painstakingly laid them into place with a lot of mortar, sweat, and hard work. All in all, I admit, I had to agree with dad when he'd say, "You know Peter, this house has a lot of character. It really begins to grow on you, if you know what I mean?"

Oh yeah, I knew what he meant. The place was actually quickly growing on me too. Who knew, but here really are a lot of things to do at Cape Lazo. I got enough experience and skills so that I could take one of the canoes out by myself to talk to the curious seals that would pop their heads up out of the water to say hello. I could walk along the beach for kilometers on end just collecting shells and stuff that had drifted up onto the beach. I could go hiking in the woods. But best of all, dad and I were learning how to sail – the hard way too, I should add.

Dad said some years ago he did a lot of sailing when he was kid. Turns out, later, he sailed a little two meter sunfish that he never took more than wading distance from the shore. We found out that there is an enormous difference between sailing the baby boat on a little lake in Quebec, and sailing Mr. Johnston's nine-meter sloop on the Strait of Georgia.

The first time we launched the sailboat, I can remember as if it were yesterday, it had to have been the most hilarious thing you could ever see. Now, I'm the first to admit that I'm a landlubber and a virtual greenhorn when it comes to sailing. Not dad. He was sure he knew what he was doing. However, when he almost capsized a sailboat that is supposed to be impossible to capsize, even dad admitted that this sailing stuff was a little more difficult than he thought it would be.

"Right dad, it's a good thing this boat's got a motor as backup," I said. "At least we'll be able to motor back to shore."

Wrong-oh. Dad, in his conservation saving wisdom, thought it best not to use the whole ten-litre container of gasoline in one-shot. So, he only put in a bit for now and saved the rest for another day. Good thinking, eh. Yes, well everyone knows sailboats are designed to run on wind power. Our problem was dad couldn't get the boat to go in the right direction using the wind. We just kept blowing farther and farther from shore. Like I had long lost sight of shore when dad decided things weren't working out and, "Maybe we should try the motor for a while."

Yes and it was great. I enjoyed all fifteen minutes of it. Happy motoring with my dad. It's too bad that when you run out of gas at sea, the gas in the can at home doesn't count. I wished he never told me about the gas he left at home. For such a smart guy he can do dumb stuff.

Did you know that the distress signal on the open sea is someone waving a lifejacket? I didn't. Dad didn't either. A couple of boats went by while we were drifting to who-knows-where. Dad and I would wildly wave and yell like crazy. The people in the passing boats would turn and wave back to us. They thought we were saying hello.

Finally, while I was down below deck digging in one of the ship's compartments, I came across the "Northwest Pacific Coast Mariner's Handbook." Skimming through this piece of nautical literature we learned the seaman's signal for distress. It worked first time. However, I wasn't too sure if we weren't better drifting aimlessly.

A crusty old fisherman who I swear looked at least a hundred years old rescued us. When we told him our story of how we came to be drifting, he tore a strip off one side of us and then the other.

"Where in hell's carnation da ya think ya are?" he screamed at us while he threw a rope over. "You wouldn't be the first pea-brains ta git killed out here on the salt chuck. A good sou'eater could blow out and then where'd ya be!"

People seldom yell at dad. People are usually quite polite, you know, he being a big shot lawyer and all. Well, our rescuer, with the overgrown walrus mustache, was anything but polite. I guess we had it coming, and believe me; our friend the fisherman didn't pull any punches as he proceeded to tow us back to shore. Just to make matters worse, once we got back to the safety of our own little cove, dad offered to pay the guy some money for the tow.

Wrong move dad. The fisherman didn't want any money. Now I'm getting worried about the old saying: A pound of flesh instead of money or something like that.

"I don't need any o' yore gall damn dollars," he growled. "Jus make sure nex' time ya know what the hell yore doing before ya head out to open water."

"Bit of a bummer, eh dad," I said as we were putting the gear away. "Think he was a Viking?" Dad felt bad about the whole thing. Dad's just not into errors. He always takes it so hard, everything is personal. He thinks you should always do the right and reasonable thing. It's just the way he looks at life. Negligence needs not happen here.

Now me on the other hand, I'm not that uptight about the odd little choke-up, providing it's nothing fatal. Ready, fire, aim – next time for sure. Might take a time or two to get it correct. Remember, the only people who make mistakes are those who don't try, or something like that.

Dad hired a gentleman who lived down Point Holmes-way to give us some sailing lessons. Dad's big on lessons. I mean the guy went to four, count 'em, universities and earned three academic degrees. So of course it figures that he'll take lessons. He was that way when he bought the motorcycle.

Our first sailing lesson was also my first introduction to David Barrington and his daughter Carin. David seemed okay, but Carin was another story. I couldn't stand her. She treated me like a dorkhead because I didn't know a jib from a spinnaker, port from starboard, or this from that. What she just couldn't seem to understand was: *If my dad and I knew all this stupid sailing stuff, why would we hire her dad to teach us?*

At any rate, we did learn sailing things fairly quickly once we got started. You ever hear the old saying: Let me show you the ropes. To me, that's what sailing is all about. A rope here and a rope there, and if (perish the thought) you should pull this rope when you should have pulled that rope; lookout is all I can say. Lower the boom was not good, and getting hit by the boom was worse.

Nevertheless, before you knew it, we were cruising, cautiously but confidently. It was great. We could really clip along the water when all the sails were set and the wind was wailing. It was scary and sensational at the same time. I couldn't remember the last time dad and I had this much fun. I mean, after a while, even Carin didn't bother me, too much. I still didn't like her, but at least she quit driving me nuts with her sailing superiority smugness.

The day ended too soon for me. However, dad offered a consolation by saying we'd set sail again first thing tomorrow morning. And to top it off, David said, "I hear some fellas say there's a pod Orca Killer whales hanging around Lambert Channel. I'll show you where the best spots are to sit and watch 'em go by."

We were invited to the Barrington's for a barbecued salmon dinner. Now the Barrington's place is about four kilometers from ours, but I've learned that out here you are considered neighbours even if you live ten kilometers apart. So be it, but I still didn't like smarmy Carin.

After dinner David brought out his maps and charts to show dad where some good whale watching spots were located.

I went outside to poke around the place. Crazy Carin, leaning on a porch post, started making weird noises up to the sky. "What is with you?" I asked, trying not to kill myself with laughter. Dad would be proud, I wasn't rude or bad mannered. Instead of laughing like a hyena, I managed to merely snort a couple of times. As I said, dad would have been proud. He always expects me to behave proper whenever we visit people, but I mean this was stretching it, to the limit and then some.

"I'm calling to the eagles," Carin said. "Don't you know anything?" She continued making the noises, and sure enough, (I still think it was just coincidence) a giant eagle flew by.

"Oh, that's the mother eagle," Carin cried. "They have a big nest over-there-a-ways in the woods."

I was going to argue that it didn't look like a female to me, but I'd never seen a male baldheaded eagle either. I really did not know the difference. "Well let's checkout their nest," I said beckoning her onwards.

So the next thing I knew we were running like maniacs into the woods. She could really run, for a girl. I mean I had to work at keeping up with her. Carin was fast and agile, too.

Anyhow, when we got to this clearing in the woods she pointed up to the nest. I could hardly believe my eyes. The nest near the top of the tallest tree in the thicket was huge, but nothing compared to the sight of the bald eagle sitting on a branch by the nest. I mean this guy was big. I didn't know birds could get that big in real life. Mind you, I had never seen an eagle before.

"See," Carin whispered softly, "that's the male baldheaded eagle. The males are usually bigger than the females."

"Right," I mean really, who was I to argue with Carin. "Hey, are you sure it is cool for us to be here," I asked with just a tinge of apprehension. "That guy isn't going to all of a sudden swoop down here and drag us up to his nest, is he?"

"Well," Carin paused and jokingly said: "They usually leave girls alone, but for some reason, eagles like to attack boys, especially tall red haired skinny boys."

Now, as I said before, what do I know about eagles? For that matter, what do I know about Carin? Other than the fact that she is a bean-brained country bumpkin who can run a little bit faster than me. Who wants to hear her stupid jokes?

Not me!

"See that nest Peter," she said pointing up, "the eagles use that same nest year after year. They keep adding to it all the time. My science teacher says their nests can end up weighing close to two tonnes."

"Take-off wuss," I told her, "I mean two tonnes!" Actually, I believed her, but I had my role to play and Miss-know-it-all knew it. However, on the other hand, I was sort of interested in hearing more. Even though Carin is a barf bag this eagle stuff was quite kewl. "What do they eat?"

"Other than certain city slickers," she said smiling, "they eat fish, mice, and all sorts of little animals they find in the forest or ocean."

"Shh, quiet," I said putting my finger to my mouth, "hear that squawking noise. What do you think it is?"

"Oh, those are the baby eagles. Didn't I already tell you about 'em," she said starting another wildlife Audubon lesson?

She told me all sorts of stuff. For example, the eagles' plumage (which means feathers to you and me, but to Carin plumage was correct) changes from baby baldies to full grown adults. The babies are brown all over; they have a black beak, dark eyes, a speckled breast, and yellow feet. Actually their feet are the only part that never changes colour throughout their life. After about five years the speckled breast begins to become solid brown. Their dark baby eyes turn yellow; and the black beak becomes a gorgeous golden colour. The brown baby head and tail turns white and that's what makes the bald-headed eagle look so spectacular.

For sure I thought Carin could be certifiably crazy, but I asked her dad later and he backed Carin up all the way. So, who am I to doubt that they watched an eagle mating ceremony? Come to think of it, it had to be true. There is no way Carin could be smart enough to make up such a story.

I have attended some outrageous weddings in Montreal, but I tell you they can't hold a candle to the eagle mating ritual ceremony. What's more, unlike most of the weddings I'm familiar with, the eagles stay mated for life. I wish dad would re-marry. He would be a good catch for someone and I good use some help managing him.

Anyhow, it goes like this: First the male and the female start flying around each other and then they begin soaring high, high, higher, circling up into the sky. When they are up so high that someone on the ground can't even see 'em, they come cart wheeling down holding each other's feet with their two-meter wingspan spread out like a falling kite. Just when it looks like they are going to crash into the sea or hit the trees, they release their grips and separate. Wow, what a wedding ceremony, eh? Mating.

As dad and I walked home from the Barrington's, the moon was shining like a big spotlight in the sky pointing our along the beach path. While we were walking up the driveway, I was telling dad about the eagles and as we got closer to the house we could hear the landline telephone ringing. If dad had his way he'd just let it keep ringing. I'm not like that.

"Hey dad," I said teasingly, "I'll race you to the phone for a sawbuck."

"You're on slow poke," dad said trying to get a head start on me.

It was fairly close, like I only beat him by a few dozen meters. I ran inside the house completely out of breath and gasping for air. As I picked up the phone, I half expected to hear a click – you know how the other person seems to hang up just as you get there. It can bother me a bit, but dad will go snake-ish over it. It's one of his hang-ups when the caller hangs up. He should get call display, problem solved. Nothing is that simple.

Instead of a click I heard Mr. Maxwell's voice. "Peter-boy," he said, "were you sitting on the white throne in the men's room or what took you so long to answer the phone. You sound like you need an iron-lung or something."

"No, I'm okay Mr. Maxwell," I replied, "I was just beating the blazes out of my dad in a foot race."

"What the hell's bells you doing racing a man who is recuperating from a heart attack?" Mr. Maxwell asked. "I hope you at least gave him a head start."

I knew Mr. Maxwell was just kidding, but actually it reminded me of how well dad was doing. Seeing him now you'd never know that he nearly died a few months ago.

It was great to hear Mr. Maxwell's voice again. We talked about all sorts of things. The big news came when he said he might be able to get away from the office for a few days to come and visit. He needed first though to talk with dad to see if it would be okay to bring a friend with him.

I could hardly get to sleep that night. I tossed and turned thinking about the eagles, whale watching, and best of all, Mr. Maxwell coming to visit.

IV.

MR. MAXWELL'S FRIEND

Mr. Maxwell's airplane was late. Dad said that's typical for the island airlines. It is called island-time. We walked around the little airport looking at the various planes that were lined in rows along the edge of thc runway. My favourite plane was a spiffy looking red Cessna. Dad liked a plain looking one called a twin engine Otter. I teased him saying that Otter ought to swim better than fly. We made Otter-mobile jokes until, finally, we saw Mr. Maxwell's plane coming in for a landing.

Compared to the airplanes we'd been looking over, Mr. Maxwell's plane seemed huge. They opened the passenger door and unfolded a little stairway leading down from the plane to the ground. When he emerged from the doorway, Mr. Maxwell looked so different. I guess I've only seen him in his three-piece lawyer outfit with the gold watch-pocket chain. I mean he looked okay and all; it's just that he looked so different than what I was used to seeing. He was wearing faded blue jeans, a plaid flannel shirt, and a fishing vest. To top it all off, on his head was a Montreal Expos baseball cap (bastards moved the Expos to DC).

"Peter-my-boy, you look terrific," he said while squeezing my hand until it seemed like my blood circulation was going to be cut off. My hand went numb. "I trust you know where all the good fishing spots are. Andrew Johnston at the firm says the salmon are huge out here. I want to join the TYEE club."

Dad and Mr. Maxwell shook hands and talked about how good they thought each other appeared until I interrupted and asked, "Excuse me Mr. Maxwell, I thought you said you were bringing a friend, couldn't he make it?" "Oh yes indeed my young friend, he made it all right," he said, "I think they are unloading him right now," as he pointed over to the plane's baggage area.

I didn't understand what the heck Mr. Maxwell was talking about. I glanced over at the baggage buggy where they were unloading all the suitcases, supplies, and stuff. And then I saw him. Sitting on top of a bunch of boxes was a metal cage containing a jet-black rolly polley hairy fluff ball of a dog.

"It's a Newfoundland puppy!" I screamed with excitement, "He's beautiful."

"That's right Peter-boy," Mr. Maxwell said. "I thought it best to check with your father first before I imported a puppy for you all the way from an old fishing village on the coast of Newfoundland."

Dad smiled and said, "Yes Peter, this is the friend Mr. Maxwell asked to bring along to give you as an early birthday gift."

I could hardly contain myself. "What, you mean he is mine," I replied. "I get to keep him," I asked.

"Only if you promise to take good care of him," Dad cautioned, "you both need training."

"Don't worry about that," I said, "I'll take excellent care of him."

Smiling from ear to ear I turned to Mr. Maxwell and asked, "Is he a he or a she?"

"Well, may I suggest we go take a closer look and let that little fellow out of his cage," said Mr. Maxwell as we walked (actually I wanted to do handsprings and cartwheels) over to the baggage claim area. There were so many questions I wanted to ask Mr. Maxwell about the puppy, but he kept smiling and said, as if he had read my mind: "I'll answer all of your questions in good speed there young man. However, suffice to say for now that you are the proud owner of one purebred three month old Newfoundland puppy."

I was so happy that I was on the borderline of crying or laughing. Thought I might pee my pants. You know how it is when you get all knotted and tied-up with the way you feel about something that is so outrageously fantastic that you actually feel like crying because everything is so awesomely excellent.

"Thank you Mr. Maxwell," I said, "He is beautiful! I've always wanted a dog but when we lived in Montreal our building wouldn't allow pets."

"Well, we have a lot of beach for him to run around at Cape Lazo, eh Peter," dad said. "What do you say we take Mr. Maxwell and your furry friend back to our place," dad said.

All the way home the puppy licked my face and we rolled around in the back seat of the car. He was so soft but he had little razor blade-like teeth that hurt when he chewed on my finger.

"We'll have to get some toys for the puppy to chew on Peter," dad said as he watched us from the car's rear view mirror.

"You can tell he is going to be one big dog when he grows up because of his feet," said Mr. Maxwell turning around towards the back seat. He was still smiling as he reached for one of the puppy's front paws. "See these web feet Peter," he said, "Newfies have these for swimming, and I'm certain this handsome fellow is going to be a superb swimmer." He shook the puppy's paw and asked, "Say is there any where to swim around this Cape Lazo place?"

"Oh man, just wait 'til you see where we swim," I replied. "Where we live the tide goes way out and the sun warms the sand, then when the tide comes back in the hot sand it makes the water like swimming in soup. You'll love it."

When we arrived back at Cape Lazo dad gave Mr. Maxwell the "grand tour" of the house, beach, and woods, while I played with the puppy. "I've got to think of a good name for you," I told the puppy as he tripped over his own big feet. I mean the guy would get going at a good clip and then all of a sudden he'd lose control and take a tumble.

I asked dad and Mr. Maxwell, during dinner, if they had any ideas about what I should name the pup. Dad said we'd be calling him swamp-rat soon if he takes another leak on the carpet. Mr. Maxwell was more serious. He explained that nautical names are traditionally given to Newfoundland's because of their history as sea-going dogs.

"Take your time Peter," Mr. Maxwell suggested, "Whether it is a nautical name or any other kind of name, it has to be one that suits him. Believe me; you will know it when the right name comes to you."

That night I made a little bed in a corner of my bedroom for the pup. Dad said he could sleep in my room while he was a puppy but we would have to build a doghouse for him when he gets bigger. "Newfoundland's should sleep outside," dad said, "because they have such a heavy coat of hair the indoors would just be too warm. Not to mention the toilet training problems we've been dealing with."

Well, I'll tell you, my puppy may have a good coat of hair, but he wanted nothing to do with sleeping on the bed I made for him, let alone the great outdoors. He wanted to cuddle with me. I let him curl up in a little ball on my bed. When I could hear his rhythmic breathing, I knew he was asleep, so I'd pick him up and place him back on his bed in the corner. I'd no sooner get into my bed when little cries from the corner would start. I tried to ignore him but then the cries just got louder. So, yes, you guessed it, he won. We were bunkmates. I couldn't take it anymore. I tried and tried to get him to sleep on his own bed. He wouldn't do it. So it was much easier to finally just let him sleep on my bed. Everything would be fine, that is, of course, providing dad doesn't find out. Because, yes, as we all know: Dogs don't sleep on people's beds. Right dad, I could hear it already. But I mean I had to get to sleep. We were taking Mr. Maxwell salmon fishing in the morning.

Looking at him lying there, sleeping like a log, I racked my brain trying to think of a good name for the pup. Nautical names. I knew

I wanted one, but I couldn't get a net over anything that sounded decent. I thought of all the nautical things Mr. Barrington had taught dad and I; all of the pirate names I could think of; and all the sailor songs I could remember. Still nothing. Finally, just before I thought I was going insane over the whole thing, I remembered about the boatswain's whistle (bosun's whistle for short) that Mr. Barrington has hanging in his den. It was the puppy's breathing that reminded me of the whistle. I mean there he was just laying there, sound asleep, sort of softly whistling air in and out of his little lungs. And that's when it hit me: His breathing sounded like a bosun's whistle. There you go, a nautical name, I liked it and, moreover, it suited him. So it was settled, we will call him Bosun.

I could hardly wait for morning to come. I was dying to tell dad and Mr. Maxwell the puppy's name. All night long I dreamed about all the great things we'd do. Bosun and I had it made. We would live it up to the hilt. Geez I couldn't remember when I'd ever felt this good before.

I have a puppy!

V.

ORCINUS ORCA

"Hey Mr. Maxwell," I shouted as our boat was heading downwind, "that's Cape Gurney over there, and around the corner is the old Hornby Island Whaling Station Bay."

"Are there any whales in that bay, Peter-my-boy?" asked Mr. Maxwell who was still smiling and quite proud of the fact that he'd already caught two Coho salmon. "Just what kind of whale species inhabits these waters?"

I edged my way down to the stern where dad and Mr. Maxwell were trolling their fishing lines. "To answer your first question: No, there aren't any resident whales in the bay right now, but that's where they at one time cut 'em up and stuff to get whale oil. Right dad?"

"In a manner of speaking, yes, that is correct," dad replied. "However, the whales that live in this area are an endangered species and it is certainly illegal to hunt them nowadays."

"Well, what kind of whales live here," I asked. "Do you know, dad?"

That was his cue. "Yes, well, now that you mention it I did a little research on this topic," he said full-knowing that I knew he'd been reading about whales in this area ever since we had dinner at the Barrington's. He had maps, charts, pamphlets, monographs and books on whales. That's my dad for you - thorough. He leaves no stone unturned. You know, like a bulldog grabbing on to something and shaking it.

"David Barrington was telling us that there are reports out and sightings of some killer whales passing through this area," dad said as he started to get in position to tell us one of his famous stories. "You know what really caught my interest about killer whales was how they have been so misunderstood by man."

"For example," he continued, "killer whales got their name from eighteenth century whale hunters who witnessed these whales tearing tongues and ripping apart other whale species that were much larger. Hence, they became known as killer whales because they killed other whales. Actually, Orcinus Orca is the scientific name for killer whales."

"At any rate, here is where we really get into man's historical misunderstanding of Orcas. You see it is true that they are one of the fiercest predators in the sea. They can swim up to speeds of fifty kilometers per hour; they can weigh up to nine tonnes; and they often measure as much as ten meters in length. Orcas are intelligent, far more so than sharks or other man-eating fish. And that is precisely the point. To this day, there has never been a documented report of an attack of a killer whale on a man. No man has ever been killed by an Orca whale!"

"How about boats, dad," I asked, "Have they ever attacked anyone's boat?"

"No Peter, there has never been any reported cases of a killer whale actually attacking anyone's boat. Nevertheless," he said with a big grin, "I'm sure that there have been some pretty anxious moments for anyone in a small boat who has come close to a pod of Orcas."

"This all sounds terribly interesting Jason," Mr. Maxwell commented, "but, what in the world is a pod of Orcas?"

"Sorry Alan," dad said apologetically, "Thought I had mentioned that Orcas travel in small family groups called pods. There is always at least one male bull Orca in every pod but other than that a pod can vary in size from seven to seventeen. This time of year they head northwards through this area up to Johnstone Strait and Robson Bight where they spend the summer. In fact, Robson Bight has the largest number of sighted Orcas in the world. And that unfortunately brings us back to more of man's stupidity. You see, a few years ago, one of the larger British Columbia logging companies wanted to turn Robson Bight into a logging storage and shipping port. Well, of course, that would have undoubtedly destroyed the Orca's summer home and probably push them even closer to extinction."

"Can they do that, dad," I asked, "couldn't you sue 'em or something?"

"Fortunately, the environmentalists have been able to hold the development off," dad said shaking his head, "So far!"

"Ah, yes, but it is a fine line we tread isn't it," commented Mr. Maxwell. "The forest industry has been the backbone of British Columbia, without it there is nothing but trouble for all who lose their jobs when the mills shut down. The last economic recession showed that quite clearly. However, on the other hand, what is going to happen if we can't get along with Mother Nature? It is not just environmentalists; we all have a stake in the future. Global warming is not a myth. There are a lot of tough questions on the docket to be answered. At any rate these issues probably will not be addressed by old gapers like me, no sir, it is your generation Peter who are going to have to strike some kind of balance between man and nature. I'm afraid sometimes that we have already past the point of no return in some places. Take all the acid rain over the Great Lakes, I'm telling you that..."

Dad yelped and interrupted as his fishing line started spinning out, "I've got a bite! Peter, get the net. Alan, have you got the fish bonker bat ready, we're going to need it? This is a big one."

"That-a-boy dad," I encouraged as he was trying to play the fish out and pull him in.

"Whew-wee," Mr. Maxwell cried, "he is indeed a big one. Don't lose him Jason."

"Did you see him jump?" I shouted. "He is at least twenty kilos or more!" I was really excited as I tried to get the net ready to grab him as soon as he was pulled to the side of the boat. "Just a bit more dad and you've got him."

Dad reeled him in a little closer to the side of the boat so I could get the net under him and I flipped the large wiggly heavy sockeye salmon into the boat. "Okay Mr. Maxwell, bonk him."

"Yes siree, its Super Salmon Supper tonight mates," dad proudly shouted, "I can taste it already."

Around about this time, Bosun, who had been sleeping below deck in the ship's cabin, started crying and barking wondering what all the excitement was about. I went below to get him and bring him up to show him his first salmon. We all took turns taking photographs of the big catch of the day. Good times for sure!

That night we had a huge bon-fire on the beach. We lit up the entire night sky. We sang silly songs, told goofy jokes about the whoppers that got away, and best of all, we ate tones of junk food.

We were having a great time, but in the back of my mind was a little sadness because I knew Mr. Maxwell was leaving late tomorrow afternoon. I wished so much that he could stay longer; the time had passed too soon. One week goes too fast.

As if he could sense what I was thinking about, Mr. Maxwell said, "Well there Peter-boy, at least we still have time for another canoe ride tomorrow morning before I have to head back to the big lights. What do you say we go chase some seals at the crack of dawn, Bosun?"

Bosun let out a little woof as if he meant to say, "Yeah, right-on, I'd love to!"

That just got us all laughing again and the more we laughed the more Bosun let out little woofs. Finally, Bosun leaped onto me and started licking my face like crazy, which of course, only made me laugh even harder.

"Peter," Mr. Maxwell laughed, "I think he likes you."

The next morning I woke at 5:00 a.m. with Mr. Maxwell whispering, "Captain, captain, wake up, the sun is shining and the crew are waiting for you. It is time for us to push off to sea." Then he put Bosun on my bed. Bosun was no help. He started in on me too. Between Mr. Maxwell trying to steal my pillow and Bosun trying to lick my face, I knew there was no other choice but to get up and face the mutiny.

Normally I am not a morning person and although my eyes hated the thought of being open, I had to admit, it was a beautiful day. The ocean looked like a mirror. It was calm, the colours and lighting were awesome. The sky, water, mountains, and even the clouds, all had a hint of reddish-orange and yellow that seemed to reflect softly in the early morning light. I usually stay in bed until a decent time of day. I mean I've never had any reason to get up with the early birds looking for worms. Moreover, like clockwork dad whips up breakfast at eight-thirty. But, if it always looked like this so early in the morning I might consider getting up a little earlier, every now and then (don't think about getting up for school because I've successfully erased that from my mind, at least until September).

Mr. Maxwell and Bosun were already down at the canoe while I was stuffing a couple of apples, cheese, camera, and binoculars into the backpack.

"Come on Peter," Mr. Maxwell shouted, "pitter patter, let's get at 'er."

We climbed into the canoe and headed straight out into the strait. Dad prefers that I stay close to the shoreline when I'm in the canoe. But I figured that seeing how the water was so calm and Mr. Maxwell here and all, it would probably be okay.

We hadn't gone very far when all of a sudden a couple of seals poked their heads up to take a look at who was doing all the splashing with the paddles. We brought Bosun with us. He loves to sit in the middle of the canoe and go for a free ride. Bosun always barks at the seals, but it doesn't seem to frighten them away. If anything, it makes more seals surface and come closer to get a better look.

"Look to the left Peter," Mr. Maxwell said softly, "there is another one behind us too."

"I see 'em," I said as I tried to make some seal noises.

"Shush, you are going to scare them away."

One seal started swimming straight towards our canoe. Then when he was about two meters away he dipped down in the water. We waited a while for one of them to surface. There was just no sign of 'em anywhere. We looked around in all directions until finally I saw some splashing in the distance.

"Hey, Mr. Maxwell," I said, pointing in front of us, "there they are. Let's go catch up to 'em."

"All right Peter my man," Mr. Maxwell replied, "put your shoulder into it and let's make this canoe fly. We can catch those buggers yet."

We paddled like crazy. We had already traveled quite a distance from shore, but now we were really a long way out into the middle of the sea. In fact, you could hardly even see the shore from where we were. However, we weren't thinking about where we were, instead, we were determined to catch up to the seals.

"There he is Mr. Maxwell," I said, "look he's laying on his side or something. A big boy, too."

"It appears as though he is floating on the surface Peter. What do you think he is doing?"

"Do you think he is dead?" I asked.

Mr. Maxwell looked carefully at the black blob-like shape that was floating in front of us. "You know it is hard to say Peter, but I don't think that is a seal. Do you?"

Just as he said that a big black and white bull killer whale surfaced not more than three meters off our bow. He was huge! His big black dorsal fin waved in the air like a sail. It stuck out of the water at least two meters. He just sort of rolled there with his big eye looking us over. Now I could see the rest of the pod had surfaced and were scattered around us, but it was the big guy who was the closest. I was scared stiff.

"That is an Orca," Mr. Maxwell whispered, "remember your father said they never attack humans."

"There is always the first time," I replied, "and besides, my dad has been known to be wrong before." Only I prayed silently that this snorting monster wasn't going to prove dad wrong.

Bosun barked, then the Orca bull made some weird noises like I never heard before and he suddenly flipped his fluke way up in the air and he slid down deep in the water. Seeing that huge tail waving high above us I was afraid he would slap down on top of us and break the canoe in half. When that didn't happen I expected a big wave to come and swamp the canoe from the splash. But there wasn't a wave or splash. He just slid into the water.

Another smaller whale surfaced just a few meters off the starboard side. "He must be a baby," Mr. Maxwell said softly, "look how much smaller he is than the other fellow."

"Looks plenty big enough to me," I said mockingly. The theoretical *baby* was more than two and a half meters long.

"I think they might be frightened of Bosun, our guard dog," Mr. Maxwell laughed in a semi-nervous sort of way.

"Don't count on it," I cautioned. However, it did seem as though they were checking us out by the way they came up close on all sides making noises to each other. They made communicative but weird garble sounds.

Then the big guy and another killer whale started doing some synchronized swimming. They threw their whole upper body out of the water and they hopped along on their tail (dad later told us that it's called spy-hopping). It was awesome; you could see their big white bellies reflecting the sun's light and their big wide mouths that uttered squeals, whistles, and an assortment of other weird noises.

The baby whale tried some aerial acrobatics but he couldn't quite get the same burst of speed and uplift as the big guys. Nonetheless, he was outrageously excellent. I mean there we were watching him do these tricks. What a show.

"They are showing-off for us!" Mr. Maxwell said excitedly, "see that one over there, watch him, I think..."

But before Mr. Maxwell could finish his sentence, the Orca he was pointing to flipped way out of the air and then smacked back down making an enormous spray.

"Eye-woo-woo," I cried, "did ya see that splash?" I fumbled with the backpack trying to get the camera out, saying "Am I ever glad he is over there doing that and not any closer to the canoe."

"You think you are glad," Mr. Maxwell added, "imagine what would have happened if the big guy did that when he was right beside us."

As if the baby whale knew what we were talking about, he came over and tried to do a belly flop like the big guy.

"Hey, get out of here," I yelled. "You are going to tip us over ya bozo!"

He couldn't make a real flop like the other big guys but he certainly made waves, which sent the canoe a rockin' and rollin'. Finally, just before my nervous breakdown, the baby whale's mother came and escorted him away. That was a close call. I mean could you imagine if we had tipped in the middle of nowhere with a half dozen Orcas swimming around us. Right, not my idea of a good time. Besides, my camera would have been ruined and I knew no one would have believed this fish story without solid evidence. And believe me; I knew I had some good pictures.

So, about as quick as they had arrived they disappeared in the distance, leaving us to the long canoe ride home.

"Hey, Mr. Maxwell," I said, just as the sight of our boathouse was coming into view, "I finally figured out where all those seals went. You see they must have known the Orcas were around. And seeing how Orcas eat seals, they split lickedly quick like."

Mr. Maxwell slapped his paddle on the water and splashed me. "Peter Mackintosh the ocean biologist we'll call you, eh," he said jokingly. "Your father is going to have my rear-end on a platter when he hears about our whale-watching in the middle of the Georgia Strait."

"Oh don't worry about dad," I assured, "I can handle him. It's all in the way you tell him the story. You have to make like it was a research project or something and he'll be pleased at our initiative."

"Research project indeed, and I suppose you are the King of Canada as well, eh," Mr. Maxwell said splashing me again. We both started laughing like crazy. Bosun, who had been curled up in a ball sleeping since the whale episode, started barking to put in his "two-bits worth." We must have been quite a sight.

I guess dad heard our arrival announcements because he was standing down by the boathouse waving. Voices travel far over water. When we got closer he cupped his hands by his mouth and yelled: "Ahoy there sailors, I was getting ready to call the coast guard and tell them you were lost at sea."

Little did dad know how close to the truth his humour was hitting.

Gawd, I was glad to see him.

VI.

PERFECT PRESENTS

Mr. Maxwell barely boarded his airplane in time. Even our little airport has check in rules. But by the time we told our canoeing whale adventure to dad, and Mr. Maxwell got his entire luggage together, we were running late. Back in Montreal dad would hate to be late. But nowadays it doesn't even faze him. He's on Cape Lazo time. That is, things happen when they happen, and if they don't there is always tomorrow.

Oh geez, but it was hard to say goodbye to Mr. Maxwell. We'd so much fun, I hated for it to all end on a dumb old airport tarmac.

"I'm going to miss you Peter-my-boy," Mr. Maxwell said as he gave me a big bear hug. "You take good care of your father and Bosun, eh. And I know now that you are going to be just fine out here in the sticks. You are a different person now than the urbanized city slicker who used to come and pester me at the office. You are turning out to be a fine young man and I'm proud to be your friend."

Guys just don't talk about loving each other. I mean what, eh, I'm going to make like the lump in my throat is a cough or something. Mr. Maxwell knew how I felt about him. But, I started crying anyways. What the hell, I was all choked-up about the whole thing. He's going back to Montreal and I'm not. But even still, I didn't really care that much about Montreal anymore. Though I sure couldn't say that about Mr. Maxwell. I mega-cared about him.

"I'll miss you too," I snorted, "and don't worry about dad and Bosun, I can handle them."

He chuckled at my fleeting attempt of light heartedness about dad and Bosun. Dad didn't really understand what we were on about, but he smiled all the same.

"You will have to return soon Alan," dad said as he and Mr. Maxwell shook hands. "I think this west coast life agrees with you."

"Oh that it does indeed Jason," Mr. Maxwell replied, "I haven't enjoyed myself this much in years. One of these days I'll retire. When I do I'll come out here and spend more time with you. Thank you for your Island hospitality."

"Our pleasure," dad said patting him on the back as he was turning to leave, "our door is always open, and as you know, we don't lock 'em out here."

Mr. Maxwell walked briskly to the aircraft and just before he was going through the little door, he turned to give a final salute wave goodbye."

Things were pretty quiet in the car on the way home. Bosun had flaked-out in the back seat and he was snoring to boot. Dad looked like he was deep in thought about something. I wondered whether he wished to be on that plane going to Montreal. After all, it had been his whole world for a long, long time. That is, until the heart-thing.

"So, do you think the silver fox will ever retire, dad?" I asked trying to lighten the load and break the silence.

He thought for a second or two, and then said, "I doubt it. Alan J. Maxwell is, before and after all else a big-time trial lawyer. The feel for law is in his blood. He lives and breathes it. No Peter, I don't think Mr. Maxwell could live without his clients, the courts, decisions, and all the other things that go with the territory."

"Well what about you dad?" I asked. "You were a work-a-holic. Mr. Maxwell said you were one of the best lawyers in the whole country."

"That is right Peter, you hit it right on the head," dad explained. "I *was* once one of the best lawyers around, but it got to me, and darn near did me in. It is in the past now. Since we have been here I have a better idea of what is important and what isn't. And I'll tell you, working twelve hours a day, seven days a week, just doesn't cut it with me anymore. There are more important things in life than winning some court case which most people could not care less about. Working day-in, day-out in a rat-raced concrete jungle isn't what I want to do anymore. For the time being, I am quite content, for once, to enjoy myself and take things easy."

He was right. I've never seen him this happy before. Montreal seemed like another lifetime ago now. You would never know that dad was a big-shot lawyer when you see him now in his overalls working on his sculptures down on the beach. Instead of carrying a barrister's bag full of law books, now he carries a chainsaw and carving tools. At first I thought he was nuts. I mean really, making statues out of logs that had drifted in from the sea seemed weird to me.

When he first got the big brain wave about carving the huge Red Cedar and Douglas fir logs into sculptures it seemed too far-fetched to turnout anything but disastrous. He started, in the very beginning, by cutting (bucking as Islanders call it) a log with a chainsaw into a bunch of stumps. The butt end of the stump he used to carve into a bust. You know, that is the head of a person with their hair, face, neck, and shoulders. He saved the rest of the log for firewood. Of course, we soon had more firewood in the middle of July than we knew what to do with. "Don't worry," dad would say, "you can never have enough firewood." He got that from David Barrington, but I knew they all say that around here.

I must admit that dad started to get quite competent with the carvings. The first few didn't look like much, but after a while they began to grow on you. Soon he progressed from carving heads to carving statues with arms, legs, and the whole works. He painted some and others he left in their natural state. Above all, dad was happier than I could ever remember. He was as busy as a bee, but at the same time he could drop everything at a moment's notice to go sailing or take a hike with me. In Montreal you could never get dad to drop anything until it was completely finished to his satisfaction. I mean the guy was a bona fide perfectionist.

Cape Lazo was perfect. Everything was going great. Bosun was growing bigger everyday; dad did his sculpting; and I had millions of different things to do. Nothing could be better, and then the bubble burst. I had clean forgotten about my annual two-week trip to visit mom and Donald. Somehow that seemed like a Montreal-like thing to do. I did not want to go to New York! I liked it here. Summer's the best time of year to be here.

I about near died when my mother telephoned. I about near drop kicked dad for being so sucky-sweet to her on the phone. I mean really, I thought he hated her; at least he could have argued that I should skip this year's trip. I did not want to go! However, trying to tell mum that I should skip the visit was like trying to put a fire out with gasoline.

I tried to tell her that I had to stay and look after dad. She wouldn't buy any of it. I tried to tell her that I had to stay to look after Bosun. She wouldn't buy that either. To make matters worse, she started trying to make me feel like if I didn't go visit I would be ruining *her* summer. I mean really, the last week of July and the first week of August are the best two weeks of the year. Why in the world would I want to visit my mom, Donald, and dumb old Ronnie? It wasn't fair.

Dad was no help. "Peter it is only for two weeks for goodness sake," he'd say.

My mother has a drinking problem. And she has problems with her temper too. She loses it all the time. Dad was not sympathetic. He didn't understand that visiting my mum and Donald was about as much fun as going to the dentist to get a tooth capped and crowned.

"Mellow-out Peter," dad would say, "you'll be back before you know it. Besides, it will do you good to catch a little culture."

Could you believe it, a guy who tells me to mellow-out also talks about culture in the same breath? Dad didn't tell people to mellow-out when we lived in Montreal.

I think just to keep things on a downward trend; dad accepted an invitation to a bon voyage party for me at the Barrington's. I do like Mrs. Barrington's cooking, but I can do without Carin Barrington constantly trying to make me look like a stumblebum. At least I know how to sail now and didn't have to put up with her sailing superiority anymore.

Walking down the beach I threw sticks for Bosun to fetch as we made our way to Point Holmes. "Dad I just know that this party is going to be boring," I said while picking up a piece of driftwood and hurling it as far as I could for Bosun to chase.

"Come off it Peter," dad replied with a note of unpleasantness (as if to suggest I was being a poor sport) "you know how you always are so certain something is going to be what you call boring, and it usually turns out to be something you end up really enjoying. Isn't that right, eh?"

"Take off dad," I told him, "you are the guy who is always telling me not to be an I-told-you-so. You know, don't point out other's shortcomings. Isn't that what you always say? Yeah, yeah, fine for you…"

"Okay, already, I apologize Peter," interrupted Mr. Perfecto himself. "Geez, I don't know how you manage to do it, but you have the uncanny knack of turning the tables so that you look like the good guy. You are the kind of kid who can fall in the septic tank and come out smelling like a rose."

"I hate roses!" I shouted, trying to get in the last word as I gave him a friendly push before taking off at top speed, "at least my breath doesn't smell like I gargle with toilet soap like a particular pooh-faced sculptor I now."

"Why you," he uttered jokingly as he stumbled to the sand.

That was all the head start I needed. I ran as hard as I could. He didn't stand a chance of catching me. That is, until bone-headed Bosun got into the act. Bosun wanted to play too, but he got tangled up on my heels and that was enough to slow me down so a certain slow-poke, middle-aged, retired lawyer-turned-log-butcher was able to catch me with a flying tackle to the sand.

Then there's the tickle treatment. Ever since I could remember, I've hated the tickle treatment. Dad loves it. Bosun thought this was great fun: me wiggling on the sand with dad on top tickling me to death.

Finally, Bosun saved me by barking in dad's ear until he couldn't stand it any longer. Dad got up and chased Bosun, but he had no hope of catching the four-legged terror of Cape Lazo. Bosun teased him by running circles in the sand around dad who was quickly running out of breath because he was laughing harder than he was running. Bosun kept yapping to announce how proud he was for saving the day for me.

While I was stuffing myself with Mrs. Barrington's delicious dinner, I told everyone how dad tried to start a fight with me. And how Bosun and I beat the blazes out of him. "We made him pay for the mistake of thinking he could mess with us," I explained. "I slugged him, Bosun bit him, and we knocked him to the sand."

Carin swallowed the whole story. I mean she believed every word. She was more gullible than the birds that leave their doo-doos on the sailboat's deck. Hook, line, and sinker, was what she swallowed? Yes sir, I had her.

When her mother said, "Dear, I think Peter is just stretching the truth a little." Carin had the gumption to make like she knew all the while.

"Oh yeah right Carin," I teased, "You just can't admit you were sucked in, eh."

Dad stepped in with his famous, "That will be quite enough young man." He always says that when he thinks I'm getting the best of an opponent.

Anyways, I had to admit it; I was enjoying myself to the max. I mean, eating great food and making fun of Carin, what could be better?

Well, I'll tell you what could be better: presents. Actually, it was the last thing I would have expected. Like it wasn't my birthday or anything, but when Mrs. Barrington came through the kitchen door carrying chocolate cake that said: "Bon Voyage Peter," I about near died. I double died when Carin and her father followed with presents. They were all wrapped with fancy paper, bows, ribbons, and the works.

"This one is from Mrs. Barrington, the baby, and me," Mr. Barrington said as he handed me a gift all nicely wrapped in paper with sailboats on it.

I ripped it open. Unlike dad, who slowly and methodically opens gifts by gently taking off each piece of tape, I rip 'em open.

Inside was a navy blue T-shirt that had a sailboat on it. Underneath the sailboat, COMOX MARINA was written in big white letters.

"If they had one that said Cape Lazo, I would have got it for you Peter," Mrs. Barrington said, "but this is getting pretty close, eh."

"Oh this is awesome," I said while trying to put it on and thank the Barrington's at the same time.

Dad shoved another present over to me and said, "This is something you've needed since we first came to the Island."

I quickly unwrapped the paper and lo and behold, what should I find but a blue baseball cap with the words Cape Lazo printed on a crest. "Custom made kid," dad said, "just so you can wear it in New York and let them know you are really a country bumpkin deep down."

Now, at this point, I guess I was getting a little watery eyed over all the commotion, but it was nothing compared to what was coming.

Carin came over and said, "This one is from me, but the big part of it concerns all of us."

Yes, of course, Carin never makes much sense at the best of times, but what could I say, eh. I mean after all she was giving me a present. I opened it to find a big book titled: Sailing Desolation Sound.

"You see," Carin explained, "this book has a bunch of maps and charts for the joint Barrington/Mackintosh cruise to Desolation Sound."

"I beg your pardon," I said politely, not quite understanding what she was talking about, but thinking it might have potential.

"What Carin means," dad said, clearing the confusion "is that we are planning a sailing trip to Desolation Sound when you return from New York? We'll go in our boat and Carin and David in theirs. We can cruise during the day and tie-up at night. So, what do you say, are you up for it?"

"Am I up for it," I exclaimed, "I can't wait to get started. Oh geez, I sure wish I didn't have to go to New York."

"Well actually," Mr. Barrington interrupted, "we couldn't go now even if we wanted. Our boat is having motor problems that we'll have to get fixed before Mrs. B. will let us go. We remember your story about when you guys set sail without motor backup. I've ordered the parts but they say it'll take ten days back order. Then it'll take me a couple of days to get everything back together running ship-shape, if you know what I mean. So there's plenty of spare time before we can get out of here. You might as well go, enjoy yourself and miss all the dirty work."

After we ate all the cake and ice cream we could hold, we cleared the table to spread out the charts and map out our travel plans. It was exciting. I felt sorry for Mrs. Barrington. She wasn't coming because everyone figured the baby was still too young to make the trip. She said babies are best left on dry land.

I couldn't help it, Mrs. B. opened the way for me to blurt, "Aw geez that's too bad, I guess that means you can't go either Carin. Your mom says babies should stay on dry land."

First she kicked me under the table and then she made the serious mistake of flicking a little bit of ice cream at me. That was it, she asked for it.

FOOD FIGHT!!

VII.

CINDERELLA'S SISTER

The airplane left Comox really early in the morning. It was one of those little commuter planes as dad calls 'em. Of course, you can't fly from here to there without a lot of hassle. It is flying after all. I mean I was looking at a three-hour "layover" at the Vancouver Airport. A layover is what the airlines call waiting for a connecting flight. I call it mega-boredom. Dad kept saying how I was going to have a "terrific time in the big apple." It takes time to get there from here.

Right dad, we've been through this a billion times before and it is just as boring now as it was before. So stop it, you are driving my crazy!

Dad notwithstanding, the best part of the entire trip was the beginning. The plane took off from Comox with the sun blasting down on the wings. We flew right over Cape Lazo, I could see our house, the sailboat moored in the water, and all my stuff scattered around the yard. Sorry about that dad, I'll tidy-up on the flipside. Then we passed over Point Holmes and I couldn't fight back the smile remembering how I pasted Carin Barrington with a hunk of carrot cake last night. Dad was mad, but what the hay, it was worth it.

I hadn't seen Vancouver Island from the air before and it was awesome. The plane began climbing high and everything looked so much smaller. It was great. I mean Lambert Channel, which separates Hornby and Denman Islands, looked like a creek from way up in the air. I wondered if this was how things looked for the eagles.

Vancouver's airport was not only boring, but also French fries and a cheeseburger cost sixteen bucks. And although I'm far too familiar with crappy food (the cafeteria in my old school sent four teachers and fifty-eight students to the hospital with food poisoning when somebody put something in the sauce that somebody else was supposed to throw out) the airport's burger tasted like the old sneaker I threw out because the rubber had rotted right off the canvas. I won't talk about the French fries because it'll make me gag again.

My connecting flight to New York was ready for boarding right when I found where they hid the video games. I mean these guys put their video games a million kilometers from where you'd expect them to be: by the washroom; by the restaurant; by the magazine stand. Nope, these guys have their video games stashed in a remote corner where nobody can find 'em. Hosers eh.

I made my way through the maze of the airport, going up escalators, down hallways, and through the security station. I was a little worried about my belt buckle setting off the alarm at the security scanner. Sure enough, deet deet deet sounds emitted as I passed through the scanner. They made me empty my pockets and try again. This time I made it through without creating a federal offence but nevertheless it's just one of those disconcerting experiences I could do without. I mean it's like getting back an exam that you should have studied harder but you thought you might maybe have squeaked through. Middle school does that to you.

The giant airbus plane taxied down the runway and I thought about the video machines again. It was kind of funny, you know when I finally found 'em and couldn't put my quarters in because the time had run out, and it didn't bother me in the slightest. I shrugged my shoulders and walked away. I mean a while back nothing was more important than video games. But now it didn't bother me to just walk away.

I did not think that I had changed since moving to Vancouver Island, but was open to the idea. I guess Mr. Maxwell was right when he said he noticed I'd matured quite a bit from the kid he knew in Montreal. I didn't know at the time when he told me, I mean I felt the same, looked the same, and thought I thought the same. You know changing just isn't one of those things you notice when you're the guy involved. It's like the day after your birthday and you don't really feel any older than you did the day before, but you're older!

Passing by the video games without throwing a spaz-attack let me know I'd changed one way or another. You see I hadn't actually played dumb ol' video games since we left Montreal. And what's more, ever since I'd been on the Island I never even thought about video games, let along play 'em. I don't know if that is what growing up is all about, but I'm sure it's got to have something to do with it. Maybe.

Many hours later, landing at J.F. Kennedy Airport, I had to laugh to myself thinking about the miniature airstrip I left behind compared to New York. This is a large town. I mean there are more skyscrapers in New York than anywhere else.

In Montreal dad and I lived in a large skyscraper and I guess back then I thought it was all right. But now I look at 'em differently. No thanks to Carin Barrington, she finally said something that actually made sense when she described her view of skyscrapers. She calls 'em "human filing cabinets" where everyone is tucked away in their little box in the sky with their number on the door. Nobody knows his or her neighbours and everybody is paranoid about everyone else. That is why they have triple locks on their doors and security systems all over the place. We don't have to lock doors in Cape Lazo.

My mum, Donald, and Ronnie were waiting for me outside customs. "Oh Peter," my mother said trying to look me over and kiss me at the same time, "look how much he has grown Donald." She started crying. She is always crying about something.

Donald isn't as mushy as mum, thank goodness. He gave me a limp handshake saying, "It is a pleasure to see you again, and I must add that you do look splendid."

"Yeah, I love the hat," Ronnie said giving me a peck on the cheek. "What does Cape Lazo mean?"

"Oh all in good time," my mother interrupted, "we really must be on our way. We have guests coming for cocktails this evening. And there is lots to do."

Ronnie looked at me and rolled her eyes at the mention of cocktail guests. I winked and smiled at her because I knew exactly what she was thinking: my mum and Donald always have guests coming for cocktails! It's their social life. My mum especially loves to hob-knob with Mr. Blah Bloat the producer, Ms. Gah Gah the actress, Joe Jerk the jazz singer, Eddie Egghead the scholar, Mr. & Mrs. Wacko, and the usual smattering of phony baloney-types who come out of the woodwork to tell my mother: "Oh what a wonderful party, we are having such a grand time." I could barf; I mean I've had more fun writing a math exam.

Kennedy International Airport is in the borough of Queens, close to Jamaica Bay Wildlife Refuge, which Donald says, is the biggest urban wildlife reserve in the world. Of course, I should have known, everything is the biggest and best in New York. Otherwise, Donald and my mum wouldn't live here. I mean these guys figure the sun rises and sets in New York City. Now I know how Christopher Columbus must have felt trying to tell people that the earth was not flat. It's the same thing trying to tell my mum and Donald that, yes; there really is life outside metropolitan New York.

There are five water-edged boroughs in New York. Donald and my mum live smack dab in the middle of the borough of Manhattan, which is, itself, smack dab in the middle of New York. They live in a ritzy Madison Avenue apartment overlooking Central Park and the Hudson River.

I love Central Park. Just as Manhattan is the centerpiece of New York, Central Park is the centerpiece of Manhattan. It is a great big eight hundred and forty acre rectangle that they created, and kept, from the nineteenth century. The weird thing about it is you can walk around in the park and really begin to think you are in the countryside or something, but that is only if you keep your eyes to the ground, because when you look up you can see a continuous high wall of brick that borders the park. It's okay though, because it's the only thing, as far as I am concerned, that makes Manhattan worthwhile.

Ronnie and I sat in the back of Donald's new Mercedes-Benz. My mom sat up front and was all in a flap about whether or not the hired help would have the hors d'oeuvres done properly and ready *on time*. Donald just kept driving, he smokes cigarettes and cigars, but not when we are in the car. Basically, Donald knows how to handle mum, just nod your head and every now and then say, "Yes dear, you are right about that."

Donald shows more wisdom than what I am ever able to muster. I always get dragged into the dumbest debates with my mum.

"Do you really like my hat Ronnie?" I asked. "Or were you just trying to bug me back at the airport."

With a faux wince she glanced over at my cap and then smiled. "Yeah, I really like it," she said, "It looks good on you. And I was serious, what does Cape Lazo mean?"

Somehow Ronnie seemed different this year. I almost liked her. She seemed much more mature not as annoying or smarmy as in previous episodes. I was so surprised to find her interested in where I lived and what I'd been doing. "Cape Lazo is where I live," I told her. "Lazo is a Spanish word meaning snare. The Cape was named by a Spanish expedition back in 1791. You see, if you're approaching from the southeast by sea it looks as if Cape Lazo is an island, but it is a trap or a snare because you could set a course and end up sailing into the shore unless you quickly realized that it isn't an island and altered your course."

"Are there any shipwrecks there?" Ronnie asked with an increased sense of interest.

"Well, not right at the Cape," I explained "but I understand that there are some nearby. I've started taking scuba diving lessons with

David Barrington, our neighbour. We are scheduled to do some dives on the way to Desolation Sound."

"Where is Desolation Sound?" she asked. "It sounds eerie, forbidding, and awfully exciting."

When we got to the apartment my mum and Donald prepared for the cocktail party, Ronnie and I retreated to the den. I showed her my pictures of Bosun, the Orcas, our house, the sailboat, and all the other awesome photographic shots I'd brought. She really liked 'em. I mean she spent about ten minutes on each picture asking questions. It practically took forever to get through the pile. And then when I broke out my new book on Desolation Sound, that was it, I mean Ronnie couldn't see or hear enough about it. It was just after 2:00 a.m. when the last cocktail guests were leaving and mum came in to tell us to pack it up and go to bed. Who was I to argue, after all, it had been a long day.

The next day was one of those where the word "muggy" came from. You know how it is when it's warm and humid. The weather just feels close and muggy. New York is like that in the summer. Muggy.

After brunch Ronnie and I were supposed to go "shopping" to get me some "decent clothes to wear."

"I just don't know why I can't wear what I've got on, mum?" I told her. "I mean there is nothing wrong with these clothes. I look all right. I'm not trying to impress anyone."

Mum got one of those looks on her face that let me know she was either going to start crying or yelling at me. "Peter," she began in a moaning sort of voice, "we are going to a premiere performance at the Lincoln Center. Everybody dresses up for the New York Philharmonic. You just can't wear jeans, and a t-shirt with running shoes to formal occasions."

"No problem Agnus," Ronnie said breaking into the spat. Ronnie calls my mom Agnus, just like I call her dad Donald. "Peter and I can go visit the haberdashery dad goes to," Ronnie glanced over my way and added, "eh, Peter."

Canadians say eh all the time and Ronnie likes to tease me about it. I didn't really mind because it was in good humour. I never thought of myself speaking with an accent. Ronnie insists I do, but she says it sounds "funky," so I guess its fine with me.

Mum couldn't believe how well we were getting along this year. We always fought like cats and dogs in previous visits. I guess we did that because neither of us was happy to have to visit New York. Fighting with each other was one way of getting back at our respective parents. I mimicked Ronnie's Southern California drawl saying, "Noooo proooooblem Agnus," and mum started to go into her peacemaker act. She was worried the ice was broke and Ronnie and I would start fighting all over again, like the good old days. But to her surprise, we just started laughing and joking with each other. Ronnie would say, "eh, eh, eh," and I'd bounce back with a "Noooo proooooblem." It was great.

Armed with a debit card, Ronnie and I made our way through the busy Manhattan sidewalks and streets. Donald buys his clothes at a fancy store that has been in business before there were any people around to wear clothes. I mean the place was old. They knew we were coming. Mum had called ahead and told them to expect us.

"Formal wear," is what Ronnie told the old guy who guided us to the section where they kept the penguin suits.

They measured me all over: my neck, waist, arms, legs, and chest. While they were measuring Ronnie was picking out things for me to try on. Then the fashion show began. I mean I tried on this then I tried on that. You would have thought a tuxedo should be a fairly straightforward purchase. You know, you find one that fits, buy it and go home. Wrong-oh. The men who worked in the store kept bringing more things for me to try on. Some were just ridiculous; some made me look like I'd won the "wuss of the week award;" some made me look like I was going to get married; some made me look like I was going to a funeral; and some just made me look like an idiot. Finally, one of the younger sales clerks brought out a leather outfit. I tried it on.

"That is it." Ronnie cried, "It is perfect. I love it!"

The old tailor who ran the haberdashery shop was very pleased that the guys finally hit on one that met Ronnie's approval. He smiled and had me turn this way, turn that way, and turn all the way around again.

Everyone seemed quite pleased with the outfit. I mean even I thought it was all right, you know, if you have to get "dressed-up." I can't say that I'd always wanted a leather tuxedo but what the hay, it makes 'em happy.

On the way home Ronnie and I stopped for a pizza. Just before I took a bite from a big gooey piece that had double cheese and pepperoni sliding off, I noticed Ronnie was staring at me. "What's with you?" I asked.

"Oh nothing, it's nothing," she replied, without the most convincing of voices that even I was able to see through.

"Take off;" I told her, "I'm not as dumb as you look."

"Peter!" she said trying to act offended.

"Ah huh, that got to you," I said smiling. "Actually, I was just kidding. I mean you aren't so bad looking and if you weren't my stepsister and all. Otherwise, I might even think you were foxy."

Shaking her head and laughing, Ronnie said, "Oh Peter, foxy? Is that what you Canadians say, eh, eh, eh? Who says foxy and since when have you started evaluating women's physical attractiveness. I thought you told me last year that you hated girls and you were *always* going to be a bachelor?"

"Hey, hey, give me a freaking break," I said, "I was just trying to be nice. You know, giving you a compliment, I mean really, geez, you looked like you had a problem or something. I thought if I said something nice it would let you know I was just kidding around when I said you looked dumb."

"Okay, okay," she said trying to swallow the big smile on her face. "Thank you for the compliment, seriously, I didn't know you had compliments in you."

"All right, lay off the bull tweed, what's your headache?" I asked. "I mean you don't have to tell me about it if it's something you don't want to talk about."

"Oh I don't know, it's no biggy," she said, "but I was just wondering, do you think your mother and my father are happy together? Like, do you think they'll always be together?"

"Heck, I don't know," I answered, "who cares, it's their lives. What makes you ask all this weird stuff?"

"Well, after all, they have both been around the track a couple times before," she said as if it was supposed to mean something to someone.

"Yeah, so what," I replied, "The sun rises and the sun sets, a few things happen in between, I don't get what the big sweat's all about. Come on; spill your guts out, what's the problem?"

"Oh, I don't know how to say this," Ronnie said looking me straight in the eye, "it's just that I've never had a brother, let alone a step-brother. If my dad and Agnus split-up like my mother and *third* stepfather, then I'll be alone again and never see you. It's like the way I never see my grandparents anymore. I miss them. I don't know," sighing softly, "I like having a step-brother. I just don't want any more changes."

"Ah geez Ronnie, are you saying your mother is getting divorced again?" I asked. "Shit bricks, didn't she do that last year?"

"Actually it was two years ago," she answered. "She has met some new guy who owns a grocery chain and lives in Newport Beach. Gawd, I was just getting used to Malibu Beach. I don't want to move again. Moving sucks!"

I felt sorry for her. Yes, moving sucks, I know, but I got over it now. I've never had any real brothers or sisters either, but I've always had Ronnie. Or at least that's how it seems. Sitting there in the restaurant, I felt very close to her.

I invited her to move in with dad and me at Cape Lazo. She said it was tempting, but it wouldn't work. She'd tough it out cuz what else could she do? She couldn't leave California life. I guess I knew what she was saying, I felt that way about the Cape. Montreal was so last year.

The two weeks passed before I knew it. We had had a lot of good times in a short time. I couldn't believe it was time to go home already. Ronnie and I had become solid, she was okay. I liked her. She has a good soul.

On departure day we all went to the airport together my flight was scheduled to leave an hour before Ronnie's. She was heading back to Southern California and I was on my way back to Cape Lazo. I was excited and anxious to get back to see dad and Bosun, but all the same I was choked about leaving New York. Ronnie and my mum, however, were mega-choked when it came time for the final goodbyes, hugs, and see-you-soons, at the departure gate. Water works and too many tears all over the place.

"Now you be sure to call," my mom said as the tears were becoming contagious and I was worried I might get 'em next.

Donald shook my hand and put his other arm around me saying, "It has been a marvelous visit Peter, thank you for enriching our summer."

Ronnie and I gave each other a big hug and I left making my way, glassy-eyed and all, to the airplane. Tears can be contagious. Saying goodbye was so sad. It just kind of leaves you with a lump in your throat. I mean you know you've got to go but it's awkward. Moreover, it hurts. I hated it, but I liked it too. I would miss them. Really, I would miss them.

VIII.

MOUNTAIN MANIA

I knew sleep would overtake me before the plane passed over the Midwest and flatlands, but believe me I tried to stay awake. I wanted to see the sights, especially the Rockies. Sitting there, nodding-off and slightly drooling, I thought of all the things that have happened since we left Montreal. I thought about dad, Bosun, Alan Maxwell, Cape Lazo, the Barrington's, and, of course, crazy Carin. Whew.

You know, even as I tell you about it, I'm amazed and certain that any psychologist in town would agree Carin was completely, undeniably, nuts. I mean she was dangerous. Who knew what she'd do at any given time?

I especially remember the time she said, "Yo, Pierre," she knew I hated it when she called me Pierre, "You want to bike ride up to the Forbidden Plateau ski resort. Riding the trails in the summer is great. You can borrow Kelsey Weissman's bike. She's gone to Victoria to visit her Grandmother, and I've got custody of her bike."

Despite the fact that there was a big part of me that was indeed very interested in going to Forbidden Plateau, especially when I recalled the legend dad described. I seemed to not even hesitate, let alone think first, before saying, "No way am I riding a girl's bike anywhere."

Now, I'm not really that macho or anything. I don't know, but I swear hanging around Carin just makes me say stupid things I wouldn't ordinarily utter. Buddha busting bozos, but I hate that feeling. Like I know it's my shortcoming but darned if I'm not going to lay the blame on Carin.

"Pierre, you doughnut," Carin said with her usual mastery of language, "There isn't any difference between a man's and a woman's bike. Especially the good ones, you are thinking about Hudson Bay bikes."

When I saw the machine in question I knew what she was talking about. You know, I always thought a girl's bike was one that didn't have a crossbar. That way they could wear a skirt and still ride. However, I should have known that that was in Montreal. Carin and her friends aren't the skirt wearing kind.

Kelsey's bike was apparently a different model than Carin's, but I wouldn't have known if she hadn't told me. The colours were the same and they both had wing-like handlebars, knobby tires, oversized disc brakes, and a quick release seat. The seat was a good deal, as I discovered later. I mean it's hard to believe Carin when she tells you things. Anyhow, she explained that it is important to be able to flip the seat lever to raise and lower the seat for different kinds of riding. For example, when you are on the highway, you want the seat up high for maximum pedaling power. But, when you are going down a mountain path you want to be able to lower your seat quickly so you can plant both feet firmly on the ground, if need be.

Right Carin, if need be.

Like most things that involved Carin, I didn't know what I was getting into until I was already halfway in it. I mean there was Carin pitching pebbles at my bedroom window at six in the morning. She likes to get an early start. So the next thing I know I'm pedaling down the road like a maniac trying to keep up to her.

KelseyWeissman's bike was all right, I thought to myself, while changing to an easier gear. Eighteen speeds! This bike had three sprockets up front and six at the back. Pedaling was a dream. Even the long and steep Lake Trail hill seemed easy. And I was more than thankful for the fat knobby tires as we were going down the gravel road beside the Puntledge River. It was uphill slow going, but a gorgeous view. We stopped at Stokum Falls for a snack.

"Yo Pierre," Carin called, "you dare me to dive off those falls?"

"Right on Carin," I said smiling, "go right ahead; let's see you rack yourself up."

I never in the world thought she was serious. I mean I don't know how far a drop it was, but nonetheless it was way more than the high diving board at my old school in Montreal. What is more, we are talking about a fast moving mountain river with rocks a-go-go.

No stopping Carin. She had her swimming suit on underneath her shorts and T-shirt, which were flying off in every direction. Before I could blink my eyes, she was making her way along the rocks to the face of the falls.

"Yo Pierre," she screamed over to me, waving and smiling from ear to ear. Then she did it. Bent her knees, tucked her head, held her arms forward, and dove over the edge. She did a swan dive – just to show off.

Ohmigod, I said silently. I could not believe she did it. All along I thought it was an act, a bluff, you know, another one of her stupid games. Who would have ever thought crazy Carin Barrington would swan dive off a waterfall.

She poked her head up through the light green foaming water yelling, "C'mon in Pierre, the water is fine."

Okay, yes, I was a bit hot from bike riding, but certainly not hot enough to kill myself diving off a waterfall. Of course, I was faced with the unmistakable fact that Carin dove without any difficulties. And the absolute last thing I wanted was to provide her with any ammunition to antagonize me with. Like saying, "What's wrong, you trying to win wimp of the week award again?"

So the next thing I knew I had elected not to give in to Carin and there I was, making my way along the rocks to the edge. No way was I going to dive headfirst. Jumping wasn't too thrilling either, but

I had to do something soon or continue looking like a statue. I closed my eyes, thought of all the things I had left to do in life, and took a running leap forward as far as I could screaming, "HERE I COME!"

I hit the water with a painful thud. It was worse than cold, I mean mountain water never gets warm. It is glacier fed water. My body went numb. I was dying, but I couldn't let Carin know, so I said, "Yowers it's a little cold Carin."

After we had been swimming for a while my body got used to the freezing water and it wasn't quite so cold anymore. Carin tried to dunk me but she wasn't fast enough and I got her instead. It was great, but after a while we got dried off and hit the road again, because as Carin said, "We don't want to get pushed for time."

Climbing up the road to Forbidden Plateau was harder than I thought it would be, even with eighteen gears. My legs felt like rubber, but I had to keep up with Carin. She was still going strong.

When we got to the top of the plateau it was worth it. The view was spectacular. You could see straight across to the mainland, Denman and Hornby Islands to the south, and Savory and Hernando Islands to the north.

"What a place, what a view," I said, as the sweat rolled off my forehead. I took in some deep breaths of mountain air. "You know Carin, this is awesome. I'm glad we came, this was a good idea"

"You think so, eh," Carin said as she grabbed the water bottle from my bike and began guzzling it.

"Hey, ya swill, don't drink it all," I said yanking it back out of her hand. But it was too late, she had killed it. I was going to do the same to her, and she knew it too!

"Try and catch me," she squealed as she leaped ahead on her bike. She blasted down the trail and I had to start cooking if I was going to catch her. Miss Deadhead Barrington was toast and she knew it. That's why she pedaled so hard I guess.

Trail riding was great. I really had the hang of it, cruising along without a care in the world. Best of all, I was steadily gaining on Carin. She started to slacken her pace and slowed down. I knew it. I just knew she was tired and couldn't hold a fast pace.

"See you later Meatbrain," I yelled pulling out to pass her.

"SLOW DOWN PETER!" Carin called at the top of her lungs, "there's a jump coming."

Too late, I found it. The hard way. You know, at first glance it didn't look like that big of a deal. I mean it only sloped up about a meter or so. It had been built for skiers in the winter to do flips and hot dog tricks off it.

The other thing that sort of surprised me was the fact that it didn't seem like I was going fast when I hit the jump. But I'll tell you I went flying high. It's too bad; I couldn't enjoy the view because I was chewing on my stomach at the time. Then the front tire hit the ground first and I followed head over heels vaulting from the handlebars.

I just lay there in a heap. At first I was sure my neck, back, and legs were all broken. However, it turns out that other than bruising my pride and backside, I wasn't too worse for wear. But I wasn't going to tell Carin, and let her off the hook easy.

She went crazy. Bending over my softly saying, "Oh Peter, it's all my fault. I should have told you sooner about the jump. I didn't think you'd actually go over it."

Carin was quite choked and I of course just had to rub her nose in it. "Ahggh," I moaned, "Oh Carin, I can't feel anything. I can't move my legs. Oh no, I'm paralyzed."

"Don't worry Peter," Carin cried, "I'll get you out of here. You'll be okay. I'll go get help."

Carin was getting quite worked up about the whole thing. I mean she was choked. And like I was biting my tongue to try and keep from laughing. Finally, I couldn't hold it any longer and burst out with a snort, which turned into full-fledged laughter.

"Pierre you creep," Carin wailed as she pounced on me slugging and poking me in the ribs.

"Hey, take it easy," I said, "I was just kidding around."

"Yeah well take this Mr. Jokeman," she said clobbering me with a pine branch. Then, she started laughing about the whole thing. I mean she went into hysterics telling my how funny I looked sailing through the air.

We both kept laughing about my future as a stuntman while at the same time trying to brush the dirt, leaves, and pine needles off me.

"The bike," I thought out loud, "What kind of shape is it in?"

"Kelsey Weissman will eat your ears if you've wrecked her bike Peter Mackintosh, stuntman," warned Carin as she went to pull the bike out of the bushes.

I was scared, but luckily and amazingly, the bike wasn't too worse for wear. That is, not counting the dirt, leaves and pine branches. Otherwise, nothing was broken or bent. They make these bikes well. I guess it's because the engineer planned the design with guys like me in mind.

We had a short rest; after all I needed to recuperate. Then we were on our way again. Only this time I went a bit slower.

"Yo, Pierre, ya crazy city slicker," Carin called over her shoulder pedaling down the mountain side, "you want to take this side road over here and stop off at the Medicine Bowls for a swim?"

What could I say? I mean I knew I was hot, dirty, and my hair had pine needles throughout, but what was I getting myself into this time? It had been a long day and I was happy to still be alive considering what I'd been through. Life with Carin was full of "side roads." However, without the slightest idea of what the "medicine bowls" were, or what misadventure she was leading me into this time, I found myself saying, "Sure, why not."

Turns out that the Medicine Bowls are these big pools in the Browns River where the First Nations Indians travelled to bath inside the cool waters. They believed the pools had healing powers or something spiritual. To get there, you have to climb down a steep hill in the valley. You can't see the bowls at first because of the huge cedar trees along the path, but you can certainly hear the water spilling from one pool to another.

I was almost falling over myself trying to be cool while hurrying to get there. When I finally saw 'em they were outrageously awesome. Four crystal clear deep river ponds carved out of the mountainside. Carin said something about glacier regression causing the holes, but like a lot of things she talks about, I just agree.

"C'mon Pierre," Carin called as she raced forward, "we can dive off the cliff up here. The water is nice and deep."

Oh great, I thought to myself, another one of Carin's challenges. But, what the heck, I felt so hot and scrungy, and the water looked so inviting that I marched up to the edge of the cliff, took a big breath of air in and dove.

Just as I was about to hit the water, the flight attendant was shaking my arm trying to wake me.

"Hello, bonjour, we will land shortly, please fasten your seatbelt."

IX.

DESOLATION SOUND

My stepsister Ronnie says I look at life as though it was some kind of fairy tale. So of course I was defensive about the whole thing and called her a number of nasty names to get even. I mean it took a while until she was able to explain it as a positive quality that is currently short in quantity with the people in her life.

"Okay, so what, yes I confess, I like a happy ending," I told her. "I don't know, I get it from my dad. You're from Disney Planet and I've never been."

My dad's a saintly sort of guy, as long as you don't cross him. I'm different, though I wish I were more like him. I mean he says you change the things you can change and try not to sweat the ones you can't change and deal with 'em one way or another cuz life is too short to be cynical about the whole thing. Or something like that.

Finally, Comox was coming into view. There was dad and Bosun at the airport to greet me when I landed. Bosun had grown bigger and dad had grown a beard. They looked great and man was I glad to see them.

"Hey dude, you're looking pretty slick," dad said with a big bear hug while Bosun joined in on chorus with a throaty style of barking.

The drive from the airstrip to the Cape is not very far; I mean it's almost close enough to walk, if you wanted. Dad was glad he brought the truck however, because I had brought back extra luggage. You know, souvenirs, back-to-school clothes Ronnie thought necessary, bike parts and accessories, and a bunch of books. Mum gave me some of Donald's old luggage to haul all my loot back.

Gawd, Buddha, and Zeus, but oh-man, it was great to be back. Ronnie jokingly says she doesn't trust air she can't see. In Southern California sometimes you can see the air you're breathing and they have issues with water quality. But here at the Cape the air, water, and everything is just great. People around here don't know a lot about pollution and I hope it stays that way.

I was dying to get back in the sailboat. I kept quizzing dad about the trip to Desolation Sound. He said all plans were in place, the Barrington's boat was fixed, and we could shove-off in a couple of days. I mean that's how long it takes dad to pack the boat with gear and groceries. I wanted to just live off the sea and eat salmon and halibut all the time, but dad thought I was too optimistic and reminded me about my eating habits. In Manhattan we'd go to restaurants three or four times a day.

The first time I saw crazy Carin Barrington since returning was in town at the local sailing shop. She looked different somehow. I don't know, I think she'd started brushing her hair or wearing clean clothes or something. She looked good. I mean, you know, she looked nice. I was going to try and tell her so, but she beat me to the punch, and then the timing wasn't there.

"Well, well, well, if it isn't Monsieur Pierre Mackintosh," she said making her way over towards me. "You look good. They must have been feeding you well. You don't look so skinny anymore." Then she put her hand on my shoulder and said, "Yeah well I remember hearing about you in a context of considerable opprobrium. I mean how could you wear your Cape Lazo cap to the New York Opera?" Then she took her hand, rubbed my back, smiled and gave me a cute little laugh, saying, "Just kidding ya, city-slicker. Nice to see you again, you're looking good today."

I was sort of thrown off stride or something. I stood there shuffling my feet, you know, dancing on the spot, trying to get a word in edge-wise but not knowing what to say. I gave a lop sided-smile.

"So, are the Mackintosh-men ready to set sail tomorrow?" she asked. "I'm picking up some parts for my dad but other than that we're out of here. I can't wait to get going."

"Me too," I replied. Like I didn't know what else to say to her. It was weird. I was at a loss for words that is until she poked me in the ribs and started bugging me about being a mountain bike stuntman.

I got out of the store in one piece and headed for home. On the way back I stopped at Point Holmes to watch some sailboard surfers. The waves were breaking nicely and the wind was just this side of wild. These guys were good too. I leaned back against a log, soaked in some sun, and found myself daydreaming about crazy Carin Barrington. She looked different today. I don't know what it was, but she looked good. Whatever, I can't explain it; it was a weird sort of feeling. But, I kind of liked it.

The next morning couldn't come soon enough for me. I was just so excited to set sail. When we got to the marina the Barrington's were already loading and preparing to set sailing. Mrs. B. was handing stuff to David and he was telling Carin where to stow it. Carin was wearing cutoff jeans and a well-worn Canucks t-shirt. She looked good. "Yo Carin," I yelled, "How are you this fine morning?" As soon as the words left my lips I wondered what-the-dingle-dorf was wrong with me. What was with the how are you this fine morning crap? I don't normally talk like that.

But it didn't seem to faze anyone. Dad was too busy pulling gear from the truck to the dock to notice. Mr. and Mrs. B. were wrapped up with their own business. So I guess I slid by on that one. And Carin, well all she did was smile, give me a big wave, and yelled, "Hey there, nice to see you, what took ya so long. C'mon, let's get going."

I thought to myself, as dad was blathering about some new synthetic rope he got on sale, what does it mean: she is glad to see me. Weird eh, cuz she has never said that before. Nice to see me, hmmm…

"Peter," dad grunted, are you lost in the ozone or what? Give me a hand with this stuff, will you."

I snapped out of my mini-trance and lent dad a hand. But still, I couldn't quite seem to get Carin off my mind. Geez, I'd never seen her wear a Canucks t-shirt before. It looked nice on her. You know, fit her well, or good colours or something. Nice neckline cut.

Finally, we shoved off from the dock. At last, we were on our way! The Barrington's let us lead the way out of the marina, so they could have a longer last wave to Mrs. B. It was a beautiful day. I mean the sun was blasting, not a cloud in the sky, and the wind was with us. This was what living is all about!

Dad and I were such a good team. We really had this act together. I mean our routines were down pat. I knew what to do, and more importantly, when to do it. Looking over at dad, I could hear him whistling his favourite tune: Doo waw diddy dum diddy doo. I'm serious; he loves it and whistles or hums it all the time. Whistling and hums are tolerable, but when he breaks out the vocals, it is an instant earache.

The mainsail, headsail, and jib sheets were full and we were clipping along at a good speed. Geez it felt good to be out here with Bosun and dad.

We had been out for a couple hours cruising northward. "Yo there mate," dad called, "come and take the wheel while I go below and get some snacks."

Bosun, who had already fallen fast asleep, snapped up and started woofing at the idea of eating. I swear he understands everything. "C'mon over here big guy," I said while rubbing behind his ears, "I'm sure dad packed some snacks for you too."

Bosun nestled his head into me and made little throaty dog-type noises. He obviously was happy to be here, and the thought of food made things even better. Ever since New York Bosun had become an eater. He was getting huge now and still growing. He looks just like a big black cuddly grizzly bear. It has gotten to the point that when he jumps up on my bed to sleep with me at night there simply just isn't enough room for the two of us. But, try and tell him that. Nothing worse than his whimpers. Well, nothing worse except dad's growls. He thinks Bosun should sleep outside at night. Actually, dad doesn't even think Bosun should be allowed inside the house at all because he gets dog hair everywhere. Of course, he says that but tell me who likes to read mystery novels by the fireplace late at night and have a big black four-legged bodyguard snuggling by him?

Just then dad's head poked up from the galley. He was carrying a tray with his world famous chicken salad sandwiches, nachos, and a brewski for him, and of course, and an extra large glass of chocolate milk for me. Even though there are times when dad tries to tell me that I'm getting too big for chocolate milk he still seems to constantly come through with a never ending supply and a life is too short to quibble philosophy. Hey, you gotta love him. Tucked under his arm were some maps, charts, and whatnot. Bulging from his pockets were biscuits and rawhide chewy sticks for Bosun.

"Hey Peter, can you still see Carin and David?" dad asked as he made his way to the cockpit.

"Oh yeah," I replied pointing to the southeast, "they keep creeping up on us." I knew that dad didn't want to get too far ahead of 'em but he also liked to lead the way without being too blatant or overly competitive about the whole thing.

More importantly, I tucked into a sandwich and grabbed a handful of nachos. Dad spread open the charts and maps saying, "We're right about here Peter," pointing to a spot on the map. "Can you see those white cliffs on the horizon starboard side? That is Savary Island. It is a banana shaped island with miles of silvery white sand."

"You want to stop there to explore," I interrupted reaching for more nachos.

Dad shook his head and said, “Naw, I’d rather go fishing, but I told David we weren’t stopping until we get to Lund.”

“Where in the world is Lund?” I asked making a mild lunge for the last sandwich.

Of course, I had to ask didn’t I, which set the stage for dad to tell me about the research he had dug up preparing for the trip. “Well Peter, we will cruise through Shearwater Passage and pass Savary Island on the west side and that is it. We will have reached the gateway to Desolation Sound: Lund. You know Peter, Lund has an interesting history. The Thulin brothers from Sweden settled in this beautiful bay back in 1889. They named the town Lund after the university town Lund back in Sweden where they had been born.”

As our boat drew nearer I could see that Lund looked like a funky little town. “There it is,” Dad said pointing to a distinctive white building with green trim around it, “That is the Lund Breakwater Inn. The Thulin brothers built the first hotel, but it burnt down. What you see before you was rebuilt at the turn of the century. And, you will be happy to hear, that your last dinner before leaving civilization is probably being prepared as we speak.”

We tied up at the dock then Bosun and I went exploring. Dad waited for the Barringtons to arrive. It was an uber-pretty sort of place. Bosun and I really worked up an appetite roaring up and down the beach. When we got back to the dock I could see that Carin and her dad had finally made it in.

We were getting ready for dinner, dad commented, “Looks like you are getting all doodled-up.” He smiled while messing my hair adding; “I’ve never known you to style your hair before dinner. You expect to meet someone here in Lund?”

“Yeah right dad,” I said flicking water at him, “get a life will ya.”

He of course would not stop smiling and shaking his head. But I could take it. “All right, we better get a wiggle on it there Peter. After all, we wouldn’t want to keep Carin waiting. Would we, ha, ha, ha,” he chortled.

He gave me an eyewink.

He looked like Sarah Palin and I know he thought she was a flake. "Take a flying leap dad," I bellowed deciding it was time to take him down a few notches. I grabbed him, playfully pummeled his midsection, and then Bosun joined in with the woof and lick-the-face treatment.

"All right, all right, you two," dad wailed, "I give up." And we rolled into hysterical laughter. Oh man this was a good time.

Carin and David were waiting for us at the restaurant. We had a nice table by the window with a panoramic view of Finn Bay to the north and Savary Island to the south. But, speaking of scenery, Carin looked good. She had done something to her hair and at first I couldn't figure it out what it was, but she did look good. Then I realized she had lost the stupid ponytail that she often wore and had let her hair fall down around her shoulders. I was in the middle of noticing the nice little sundress she was wearing when dad elbowed me in the ribs whispering, "Don't stare."

Dinner was delectable. I mean these guys knew how to cook a salmon. Dad and David chitchatted making plans for tomorrow. We had already established that the entrance to Desolation Sound was eleven kilometers from Lund and therefore a 7:00 a.m. start tomorrow would be appropriate. So while they had a second cup of coffee, Carin asked, "Hey Peter, want to take a walk down to the beach."

"Ya sure," I replied, "That's a good idea."

As I was stumbling out of my chair I caught dad's eye winking with a willful smirk he said, "Keep your eyes open for submarines." That was code. I remembered he told me how he used to take his girlfriend in college "parking" to watch the submarines. What that really meant was that they were there to make out. I knew these things.

Bosun lay sleeping outside the restaurant. I sort of thought it might be an idea to try and slip by him and stroll down the beach as a duet, not a trio. Not a chance. As soon as Carin saw him she cried out softly, "Bosun, you big lug, get up and c'mon down to the beach with us."

The big guy was shaking off some sleep and starting to come alive when one of the cooks appeared with a huge bone. I mean this was the kind of bone my vegetarian stepsister would gag over. "May I?" asked the cook. Of course, Bosun gave the reply. I just smiled as Carin grabbed my hand and we started running down to the beach. I glanced over my shoulder and could see Bosun hard at work on the big bone.

Anyhow, the night was beautiful and I have to admit Carin was too. I mean the way she looked in the moonlight was really something. There were some slippery rocks so I extended my hand for Carin to hold onto in order not to slip or anything. We strolled arm in arm down the moonlit beach and I was giving her the same speech dad had given me about how Captain George Vancouver had been unhappy with the area naming it Desolation Sound because of the isolation when all of a sudden she put her arms around me, looked me in the eye, and slowly planted what I will always remember as the first real kiss in my life that counted as a real kiss.

I lay in my cot that night thinking about Carin. Whoa, what was the deal here I wondered. I mean really, this was a new sort of thing for me. Weird, but I liked it. Sort of like one of those "magic moment" type-things my dad talks about. I mean this Carin thing was not that big of a deal? Like my dad talks about when I was born as a "magic moment" or the day he received the Canadian Lawyer of the Year Award. That was a really big deal for him. I didn't understand all the fuss and hubbub, but I knew Lawyer of the Year was a big deal because I had to get dressed up in fancy clothes. And I mean everybody came to this gala. Even my mum and Donald sat in row three. And I thought they hated dad, and he hated them, but refused to admit it or talk to me about it.

I'm never getting married. So of course divorce will never be an issue for me. But adult stuff is weird to think about. You know, like who does what and why just isn't that big of a deal to kids my age. I don't know, sleeping on the boat is nice. I like lying in my bed with a gentle rocking motion. Sometimes at the Cape when dad is feeling mushy, we cuddle on the big leather rocking chair and rock slowly. We have always done this, even now when he says I'm getting as big as a moose. Geez, but Carin Barrington did look good today…

Morning came with the sound of dad's familiar whistling and the smell of breakfast. The four of us ate quietly. Dad and David talked about the meaning of life, politics, and other such things while it seemed as though Carin wouldn't even look my way. What, was last night nothing to her? Then our eyes met and she winked at me. Geez, first dad, now her. Winking, what a thing eh. Who started these types of things and what does it mean when someone winks at you?

X.

SQUIRREL COVE

I love to lie on the deck up at the bow. These days laying in the sun soaking up rays is not, as dad says, prudent. But it feels good. However, skin cancer should be avoided. I know that. Hey, I try to use lotions, sunblocks, and creams.

The First Nations Indians believed the sun was like a god. Made sense, you know, like how the sun gives life and all. The pygmies believed the sun, forest, and rivers were all gods to be respected. I think I'd like to be an anthropologist. That would be a cool job.

Oh, but this is the life, just lying here soaking in the sun. This has been the best trip of my life. We've had so much fun. So many adventures. Exploring Prideaux Haven was spectacular. Mind you, skinny-dipping with Carin at Cassel Lake was pretty exciting, if you catch my drift.

You see Cassel Lake has this waterfall that drains into Teakerne Arm. Carin and I took the zodiac to shore and went hiking while dad and David moored the boats and had a siesta. Anyhow, a long story made short, we got quite hot hiking, and oh how the water in Cassel Lake looked so cool. Carin suggested swimming. I said I didn't bring my swimming suit. "No problem," Carin suggested skinny-dipping.

She'd brought her birthday suit. The next thing I knew Carin had peeled off all her clothes and dove off the cliff into the water.

What do you expect? Of course I followed. I mean really, what you think I'd sit there and watch.

Anyhow, we were headed towards Squirrel Cove. That is where it all happened: Squirrel Cove.

Well maybe I am getting a head of myself here. It started just off Joyce Point on West Redonda Island. The Barrington's boat had broken down. While David and dad did the repairs, Carin and I took the Zodiac to explore the shore.

While we were hiking all over the woods we met a family of Klahoose First Nations Indians. They were camping in the area. Historically, generation after generation of Klahoose Salish Indians came to this place called Texem Taajim. Translated, it means "red cedar place." They gather cedar roots to make ropes and baskets.

Carin and I offered to help. They gladly took us up on the offer. Henry, the oldest boy, showed us what to do. It was hard work, but it was also fun. While we were working the grandfather told us stories that his grandfather had told him.

Time rolled on and we had to get back for dinner. David and dad don't mind us exploring, as long as we are not gone too long and return in time for dinner. You know, these are the basic ground rules.

We were anxious to get back to the boat to see how the repairs were going and to tell 'em about our afternoon's adventure. After listening to some of Henry's grandfather's stories about Squirrel Cove, Carin and I were convinced we had to go check it out. Of course, we would have to convince David and dad too, but hey, we were good at talking them into things.

"Yo, prepare to surrender;" I yelled as the Zodiac approached the sailboats, "we're coming on deck." But I don't think they were all that impressed. Dad just gave us a half-hearted wave.

"Hi Carin, yo Peter" dad said, "We've managed to fix the cap shrouds and bumper stays. So we can sail tomorrow."

We tied the Zodiac to the stern and began telling 'em about Henry, his grandfather, and Squirrel Cove. Dad looked quite tired or something. I don't know, he isn't big on boat repairs, I know that much. He is not a hand man. Anyhow, he said he was tired and had some aches and pains but nothing a good dinner couldn't fix.

Carin and I agreed and set to the dinner preparations. We each have our respective chores. Mine is place setting. Hard one to screw up on, eh. Yes, well that is why they gave it to me.

All through dinner Carin and I talked about going to Squirrel Cove. Henry's grandfather had told us about a great saltwater lagoon where the water flows in and out with the tides causing rapids in between the lagoon and Squirrel Cove. The Klahoose First Nations Indians would have races shooting the rapids.

"Henry's grandfather makes it sound so exciting," I explained, "We've just got to try it."

"So you want to have some races, eh," David said, "I've heard of this place before, but have never been there." Looking over at dad, David gestured, "I'm game, what do you think Jason?"

Dad scratched his head, smiled, and slowly said, "Well why not."

"All right," Carin and I shouted, giving each other a high five, followed by respective eyewinks.

Bright and early next morning we set sail in our respective boats. It was a definitely a decent day with good winds. Our bright orange and blue coloured spinnaker sailed us down Lewis Channel and over to Cortes Island in no time flat. We cruised into Squirrel Cove together as a flotilla. Well, there were our two boats together and as far as I'm concerned that is a flotilla.

We dropped anchors and the Barringtons rowed their inflatable dinghy over to our boat.

"Ahoy there sailors," I shouted as they drew up to our stern, "toss me a line and c'mon up."

After some brief chitchats, we got started about who is going with who to shoot the rapids into the lagoon. Timing is everything most times, but particularly for shooting the rapids in a dinghy. We wanted to be riding in as the tide was changing from low to high. You know, the tide's ebb and surge stuff. "The high tide is coming is coming in soon." Mr. Barrington said, looking up from the tide table chart.

"So dad, you think you old guys might want to race?" I asked, "Carin and I challenge."

He doesn't like being called an old guy. So of course the next thing I knew there we were perched in our respective dinghies waiting for the exact moment when the tide was changing to race. Dad and David tried to psyche us out by saying this was like riding a sleigh, the heavier you are, the faster you go.

"Yeah well no doff eh," I replied, "you guys got some weight all right, but we have paddles." And with that Carin and I took off paddling like crazy.

The bay was nice and calm, but I could see the rapids just up a bit ahead of us. I looked over my shoulder and the old guys were right on our tail paddling hard.

Both dinghies hit the narrow rapids simultaneously. Carin and I were still paddling as hard as we could. Hey, I've been paddling a canoe all summer; I know how to paddle hard. Casting a quick glance sideways I could see dad and David paddling to beat the band. And then all of a sudden, like a blur, I saw dad drop his paddle and slump his head down.

I tried to keep 'em in sight but now we were going too fast. The next thing I knew Carin and I spilled out of the rapids into the calm of the lagoon. Something was wrong. I could feel it, but I couldn't see their dinghy for what seemed like forever and a day.

David burst through the rapids screaming, "We need help!"

"Dad, dad," I yelled. "David is he okay?" I pleaded.

And from my eyeballs to the pit of my stomach, all I could see was David Barrington shaking his head to say NO. "Something is wrong Peter," David said coming along side our dinghy, "we've got to get help fast. He is having a heart attack."

Dad was lying in the boat in a pile. He looked up at me. He couldn't talk, but he gave me the old thumbs up sign.

"Don't worry dad," I cried, "you'll be okay. I'm going for help." The only thing was I didn't know which way to turn, where to go, or what the hell to do. I mean I knew I had to radio the Search and Rescue, but how? Our radio was back on the sailboat on the other side of the rapids. Cell phones won't work out here, no coverage. I started looking all around us. I was frantic and in a panic, but in the corner of my eye I spotted an old man in a powerboat trolling for fish.

Carin and I started paddling towards him yelling our heads off. As we got closer we finally got his attention. But he couldn't understand what all the commotion was about until we had drawn along side his boat and slowly explained the situation. The old man fortunately had a radio on his boat and sent out a mayday call to Search and Rescue.

Meanwhile, David had paddled to shore. When Carin and I reached where they had beached I could see that dad had lost colour. He was turning a bluish white kind of colour. I didn't know what that meant, but I was starting to get really worried. He was unconscious.

For what seemed like an eternity, but actually was only twenty-five minutes, the Search and Rescue team's hovercraft arrived. They started working on dad immediately. Whoever was in charge called in a helicopter to airlift dad to the nearest hospital in Campbell River. I was in shock. Like I knew what was going on but it was just so blurry and weird.

The helicopter arrived. It didn't land because there was not enough room and it was faster to lower a basket type stretcher that they put dad on, raised him up and took him away. I had wanted to go with him in the helicopter, but he was gone before I could explain. So I was taken to Campbell River in the hovercraft.

When I got to the hospital dad was out of surgery and in the ICU (Intensive Care Unit). I couldn't go in to see him and nobody would tell me what was going on. I didn't know what to do. I found a pay telephone booth and called Mr. Maxwell. He should know what to do, but he wasn't in the office. I left a message with the secretary saying Peter Mackintosh called. "Tell him my father has had another heart attack and is in the Campbell River Hospital."

Old man Maxwell got my message all right because he was at the hospital by morning. He had chartered airplanes and had flown in the A-Team. Dr. Leonard had come from Montreal and he had called in his colleague Dr. Swanson from Los Angeles.

Valiant attempts, but dad died anyways. He had hung on for a while. There was talk of heart transplants and artificial hearts and stuff like that but he died before they could do anything. He wasn't strong enough to last longer and even if they had a donor heart available dad wasn't strong enough to receive it.

I was sitting in the hospital cafeteria when old man Maxwell broke the news: "The doctors did all they could Peter." He put his arm around me trying to comfort me, but it was no use. I went beserko.

Like I knew it wasn't his fault or the doctors. But I was pissed off big time. This wasn't fair and I let the world know. "Shit, fuck, suck, muck, yuck," I cried bawling my brains out. I threw some dishes, kicked some chairs and screamed for a while. Then I stopped for a couple of minutes and then started all over again. It was like the more I thought about it the worse it got. I hurt all over and then some more on top of that.

XI.

GOING HOME

The next number of days, and long lonely nights were sort of blurry and awfully miserable. I of course had no idea things could get any worse than they already were. But they did.

My mother arrived in a large flurry and great commotion. She wanted me to move in with her and Donald. I did not. My stepsister Ronnie wanted me to come and live in southern California with her people. I said I'd think about it. The Barringtons wanted me to move in with them. I definitely didn't want that. I mean, I liked them and all that but I certainly didn't want to be Carin's new stepbrother, half-brother nor her husband or whatever it is when you live in the same house.

But hey, on the other hand, don't let me try and fool you. I am thirteen years old. This means that although I am not a child, I have no say in anything and everyone treats me like a child.

The thing I remember the most and seem to just keep churning over and over again in my mind is my dad slouched in the dinghy giving me the old thumbs up sign. Like why did he have to go and do that? You know I can't even remember his last words to me only the thumbs up sign. And when I look backwards I could have seen the whole thing coming. It just wasn't anything I was expecting. Thumbs up all right.

Dad didn't like funerals and that sort of stuff. I knew that because he had told me. Trouble was that he had never told anyone else. And telling me meant nothing because I am in charge of absolutely nothing. Everyone seemed to be making all these stupid plans and telling me: "It is what your father would have wanted." When it wasn't but they thought so. So that is how it would be.

Things just kept getting worse. And there wasn't anything I could do about anything. Dad had always been the boss. Nobody ever messed with him. So you see until dad died I had never had any reasons to act assertive. That was dad's job. And now that he was dead everyone figures that it is now his or her job.

Old man Maxwell warned me to expect a few problems and lots of advice from lots of people. This isn't verbatim or anything, but basically he said: "Peter, everyone is going to tell you everything they know about death because everyone knows someone who has died."

Maxwell was right. I mean everyone had something to tell me. All I wanted was to be left alone with Bosun. Not too likely eh, I'm only thirteen years old. Therefore, everybody gets to boss me around and tell me where I am going to live and with whom. The thing was that I didn't want to live with anyone. And I certainly didn't want to go anywhere.

But you know, this story does get a bit better, in a way, I guess. I mean just when I thought things couldn't get any darker, a ray of light suddenly shone through. I was sitting on the beach with Bosun when Maxwell ambled down to chat.

"You know Peter I love it here at Cape Lazo," he said with a smile, "I'd like to retire here with you and Bosun. That is, of course, if it was okay with you two."

At first I didn't really know what he was talking about. But then it all started coming clear. He had been making arrangements and negotiating with my mother and all the others who thought they knew what was best for me. You know, "It is what your father would have wanted," type thing.

Maxwell didn't want to be my dad. Nobody could ever replace my real dad. Maxwell had made arrangements to be assigned as my legal guardian. He wanted us to stay at the Cape. He wanted me to go to school, university, and the whole gamut. I didn't have to move. Bosun and I could just stay here.

So of course, that is what we did.

XII.

EPILOGUE: SEVEN YEARS LATER

The thing about rural island life at Cape Lazo is it does not change much. How it is now is pretty much how it was ten, twenty, or who knows how many years ago. Time warp, I guess. People change. Generations come and go. But Cape Lazo stays the same. And of course, some level of stability in this crazy life is always welcomed.

Last year, Maxwell and I went back to Montreal. He was receiving the Order of Canada award from the Governor General. It was a really big deal. The Governor General seemed like a nice lady, and there was a whole lot of hubbub, too.

We both bought new suits at Harry Rosens for the formal soiree, and semi-casual duds for the post award festivities. It was, as Carin's little brother, Daniel, incessantly says, "All good."

Montreal has changed. A few things were the same, some buildings down, others renovated. And another referendum on separation had come and gone, too.

Some of my old friends were still around, and it was great to see them. My old friend from elementary school, Wes Sorokin, and I managed to make it to lunch. We met at a funky little restaurant at the Chateau Versailles Hotel.

Wes looked pretty much the same, older, a bit heavier, but pretty much the same. We were on our second beer when Wes says, "Peter, it is amazing man. I haven't seen you in close to seven years, and you haven't changed at all."

Yeah, that's the thing, eh. There have been some changes in the last few years, but as far as Wes was concerned, I hadn't changed a bit.

Crazy Carin Barrington will never change! I have always known that as a metaphysical constant. "You can take to the bank," dad would often say.

After Desolation Sound Carin and I were more or less inseparable. We were soul mates. You could call it puppy love, young love, first love, lovebirds, or whatever, but we were wonderfully in love or some semblance thereof "at our age."

Of course, Carin could fight, too. Given Carin's sometimes-synonymous streaks of stubbornness and stupidity. And I am not referring to the PMS either. I learned to recognize the symptoms and tried to not get sucked into an endless power struggle with Carin's adolescent mood swings.

Individual differences are important. There are introverts and extroverts and a whole host of people in between. Quiet people, however, make Carin nervous. "Who knows what the deal is with them," she would say, "They don't talk to you."

High school with Carin's company was a lot like Janis Ian's song; "I learned the truth at seventeen." It was a wild and wonderful time, especially drafting behind Carin Barrington's lead. She was a force to contend with and never shied from controversy. I loved it and hated it, too. It was a time of life like no other. At least that is what I thought until graduation and our transition to college.

While we were in our senior year of high school we applied to a few universities, but our first choice was the University of British Columbia in Vancouver. We worried about entrance requirements, supply and demand, too. Everyone wanted to go to UBC and not everyone gets in, but we did.

We both got acceptance letters the same day. The anticipation in opening the envelope was too much to bear. I couldn't do it. Carin opened mine and I opened hers. We had a big celebration dinner with all the trimmings and toasts.

UBC was huge compared to Comox. UBC had more students than our whole town and neighbouring towns put together. It was great. I liked the urban lifestyle. I liked the Profs. I liked the classes and I especially liked going for tea to talk anthropology, sociology, economics and philosophy. I loved the humanities, couldn't get enough.

Carin was into science. Her passion, since birth it seems, was biology and environmental sciences. More specifically, Carin started studying oceanography.

For the entire amount I started to love life at UBC it all started to become bull tweed for Carin. She thought the other students lacked passion and were sellouts to the establishment. She thought the Profs were biased pawns of corporate bourgeoisie who were polluting the earth and ocean.

A critical incident, a breaking point, or the straw that broke the camel's back was the day she discovered Orca whales were soon to be on the list as on the brink of extinction.

She came flying into my dormitory room waving a photocopied research article that demonstrated "empirical proof of what is going on with the whales."

Often my dad would say, "Once you squeeze the toothpaste out, it is awfully hard to get it back into the tube." He also stressed that we must be the caretakers of the planet. His generation and the previous generations had done a good job of global warming and basically screwing up the planet. I don't know dad, but I think the band has already left the stage and packed the instruments away. Elvis left the building. Maybe it is too late; maybe the planet's paste has already been squeezed out. But, hey, sorry Carin that is just the way the world turns. And I guess life goes on until it doesn't go on anymore. When dad died I thought the world ended. Certainly it ended for him and even though I cried for days the sun kept coming up anyways. So what would I know, you just learn to roll with it, and you just let it happen. The sun rises, the sun sets, and a few things happen in between.

Carin got all caught up with earthquakes, too. It is true we live in an earthquake zone. The Pacific Northwest is ripe for a whopper earthquake. I have always known that it could happen today, tomorrow, next month, next year, or in another two hundred years from now. What can you do, eh? That is just the way it is and life goes on until it doesn't.

Freshman year, three quarters through, somewhere around the spring break, Carin quit university and took off without saying goodbye. She broke my heart.

I spent spring break skiing. Carin went underground with some group of environmental militants she had met at a peace rally. It really did not make much sense to me, but there are a lot of things I do not understand. Carin was always one of those things that were hard to understand. And that was Carin Barrington.

At first we kept in touch with phone calls, email, cards and letters, as well as parental reports from the Barringtons whenever I was in the Cape Lazo neighbourhood.

Once I saw Carin on the television news while preparing dinner. I was chopping onions (and that is why my eyes watered-up) when I heard her unmistakable voice and familiar banter. She was the spokesperson for a group protesting corporate pollution. They had hung a huge banner across the Golden Gate Bridge. Carin had become a professional protestor. But, she was always the same Carin Barrington from Point Holmes to me.

We tried to rendezvous when her mother had her fiftieth birthday party. Carin came up early from California and tried to coax me over to Comox. I had midterm exams and could not abandon ship as fast as she wanted and then when I was able to get over to Comox, she was already gone. There was an oil spill in Alaska and she had to go to help clean seabirds coated with crude.

So, I guess that is how it goes. Dad always said, "It is a long season, pace yourself." Mind you, he would also say, "The race does not necessarily go to the swiftest, but those who keep running."

Carin, Ronnie, and Maxwell were anchors in my life. And that is how it goes, but just like sailing the Sloop, one must weigh anchors, so: Heave ho, here I go.

I am looking forward to the ports of call down the bend and around the corner.

PART
TWO

I.

SOCRATIC SYMPTOMS

After earning a degree in anthropology, I traveled a bit, and I worked at some odd jobs. You know, driving cabs, delivery trucks, construction, and one winter I worked as a ski lift operator in Banff. After my money ran out, I found I had also run out of ideas of what to do next. So I went home. It was high time anyways. Its not that I was at a dead-end or anything, but I wasn't going anywhere either. Just treading water; dancing on the spot; running in a circle; guess I was just between endeavours, or something of the sort.

Well, with that in mind, I thought law school could be my next option. Why not? At this point it was what everyone else had always expected. "He'll come around in time," they would say. So sure, I could give it a try. My life has always been too full of lawyers! My father, the well renowned and certainly famous jurist, Jason Martin Mackintosh, was my early introduction to the law.

Dad died when I was thirteen. It was the worst time of my adolescent life. However, it was also the beginning of a rocky relationship and enduring growth period with my legal guardian, stepfather, and main mentor (and at times we put tor in front of mentor as he could torment as well as mentor), Alan K. Maxwell, Q.C. who was a senior partner at dad's law firm. After dad's death, Maxwell retired from the practice of law to try his hand at raising and dealing daily with a crazy but sometimes lovable teenager.

Oh man those old lawyers and I had some times together. I was born in Montreal, and lived with my dad after my parents divorce. We moved to Vancouver Island after his first heart attack. Basically, I grew up at Cape Lazo. Of course, that is, if one were to think of me as having grown up, graduated, and on the other side of the "formative years." So to speak, eh. As an articling law student I remember parking next to one of the firm's crackerjack lawyers whose Porsche bumper sticker said: You are young once, but you can be immature forever! I never made crackerjack status, but for the longest time, practiced the motto.

Sitting here now, watching the waves wash over the sandbar in front of our rustic old beach house, with the rain tapping time on the bay windows and dormers; I can certainly retrace the whole thing and put it in context. Reflect and recognize events as they had unfolded. Still, all in all, it is quite a saga...

ANNIE JARMAN AND SOCRATES

I first met Annie Jarman in the parking lot on the first day of law school. Funny, but she always had this annoying habit of parking, or should I say abandoning, her car almost anywhere she wanted. It just was not a problem, to her. Trouble was, of course, although the Campus Patrol Officers at the University of British Columbia may not hold a high level of arresting authority; they do know how to call a tow truck to remove improperly parked vehicles.

Walking towards my Jeep, I could see Annie waving her arms, gesturing, and generally pleading her case to an elderly Campus Patrol Officer and a rather large, on the other side of unsightly looking, tow truck driver. I recognized her right away as the vociferous know-it-all who sat two rows in front of me in Professor Sheppard's Contracts 202 class.

"Gentlemen, could you pleazzze give me a break just this one time," Annie said in the most cajoling but nauseating voice I hadn't heard since junior high. "I know I made a mistake parking here. I promise that I'll never do it again. It was a mistake and I have learned my lesson. Honestly, I am very, very sorry."

Thought I'd about near hurl. I couldn't cope with her charade, but of course, it worked for Annie. I mean is it not just disgusting or what? Annie's cute little sports car is attached to the tow truck and ready to roll. Yes sir, it is off to the UBC impound lot. But no, wait, not quite, an endomorphic lady at the microphone yet. Yes, Annie shows up in the nick of time, batting her big green eyes, flashing that perfectly orthodontically corrected preserved toothpaste smile, and convinces "the guys" to "give her a break."

So there you go, no ticket, no tow, but hey, she did get a verbal "*WARNING*." Oh yeah, I can relate to a verbal warning. Recently, I parked downtown, apparently in an illegal spot. I returned just as the tow truck was beginning to attach my Jeep. I, too, pleaded my case --without whimpering or whining- I should say, eh. But the rule is: "Once we have arrived, we have to complete the call. The vehicle is effectively impounded." Pay now, plead later.

I could use a break. No way though, it became a FIDO situation. That means, (F)orget (I)t (D)rive (O)n. Tomorrow's another day. Just let it go and drive on. FIDO

First day of law school walking to my Jeep I just shook my head about Annie's form of justice. It had been a long day, time to hit the road. I climbed in, turned the ignition, only to hear another nauseating sound to compete with Annie's call-of-the-wounded voice. My battery whined its way to a death knell. I guess with the low grade anxiety of the first day of law school, the excitement of securing an excellent parking spot, I had bailed out, locked to doors, jogged to class, and left the old Jeep's flipping headlights shining.

"Damn," I said a bit too loud while thumping the steering wheel, "this is just great!"

Just then, Annie Jarman rolls up in front of me calling out, "Any problems?"

You know it has always been excruciatingly difficult for me not to act like a butt-head or at a minimum reply with a condescendingly smart aleck smarmy type of comment that invariably always proves less than helpful. I'm not a know-it-all Paul. This is something I have known for a while. And, yes, I am working on it. But, hey, these things take time, a lot of time, too.

"No probs here luv just can't catch a freaking break, do you have any jumper cables," I asked as politely as I could --bearing in mind my personality predilections in spoken discourse with damsels in distress.

Annie just shook her head with a smile and a cavalier wave-like gesture saying, "C'mon, get in, I'll give you a lift to the gas station outside the campus gates."

So there I was climbing into her car, "Thanks," I extended my hand with a friendly tone saying, "I'm Peter Mackintosh."

She returned a firm handshake, still smiling, and said, "Hello there Peter Mackintosh, I am Annie Jarman. You look familiar, are you a law student?"

"Yes," I snorted, "I'm in Professor Sheppard's Contracts 202 class. I sit two rows behind and three seats to your left." You know first year seating chart and all that sort of posterior positioning.

"Oh yeah, that's right," she said, "I remember now. You are the Mr. Mackintosh that did not think pontificating whether or not the facts were relevant in Regina vs. Wong. Hmm, what were your words? Oh yes, I believe you said that irrespective of those facts the contract was valid considering the long legal tradition established in Maxwell vs. City of Montreal."

I managed a contrite smile and was going to tell her how I was actually in the courtroom observing the case when I was a kid. Trouble was I could not get a word in edgewise. I sat there thinking, this woman is a bit too much.

"What a brown-noser, eh," she said while flipping her perfectly coiffed auburn hair, "how did you come up with all that stuff? What, were you pre reading and studying all summer or something?"

Again, attempting to get a word in edgewise and disclose some personal history. I started to try and say, "Actually, Annie, I was present in the court when.... HEY, watch out, didn't you see that pedestrian? In the crosswalk, no less," I screamed, pointing at the man Annie almost took out of the game of life.

"Relax Mackintosh," she chortled, "that wasn't even close."

"Geez, Buddha-baby, Annie, you drive like you park," I replied, "with complete utter abandonment."

"Get a grip on reality pal," Annie said shifting gears, switching lanes, and horning a cyclist, "you even talk like a lawyer. Lighten up, eh."

I just smiled, tightened my seatbelt, and sat there wincing as we went down the wrong side of the road for half a block. You know how this goes—she was just taking a shortcut into the gas station. Climbing out of the co-pilot's cockpit of Annie's car, I thanked her for the ride and was trying to tell her how I appreciated the help, but it was just too hard for Annie to let me finish a complete sentence. I was trying to tell her about how great my future was going to be if only I could live long enough to finish the story.

"Say Mack," interrupted Annie, as she fumbled through her Gucci purse pulling out pen and paper, "we're throwing a little back-to-school soiree at my friend's place tonight, C'mon over around nine-ish," she said with a wide smile.

The next thing I knew Annie tossed me a royal-like wave, put the pedal to the metal, and peeled out leaving me standing there without a rebuttal. There was no way of getting a word in edgewise with that woman! Leaning on the gas pump, looking at the crumpled piece of paper in my hand, I had to smile and shake my head in wonder.

"You okay son?" asked the grandfatherly looking gas station attendant.

Sliding back to reality, I replied with "I've had better days. It appears my car has a dead battery back at the law school parking lot."

Great gas station attendant; he waved to the redhead inside and yelled, "Handle the pumps Donny, I'm headed over to the U to give this guy a battery boost."

There were two tow trucks at the side of the shop. A modern looking super-duper machine and an old rickety Ford tow truck that was undoubtedly manufactured prior to my date of birth. And of course, the old guy gestured towards the old-mobile saying, "Hop in son, this is my Baby Bertha. Nice truck, eh?"

"Yes siree it's a beauty," I said with a smile. For the first time today, I finally felt at ease, despite the fact that I was bouncing around in the truck's cab on my way to retrieve the Jeep. I liked the old guy. He had a nice way about him. Besides that, he drove better than Annie, by far. "Thanks, sure appreciate your help. It's been a tough day."

"You new in town son?" he asked kindly.

"Yes, I'm from Cape Lazo on the Island," I replied, "and today was day-one of law school."

"Nice looking young lady who dropped you off in that fancy little sports car. Is she a law student, too?"

"Yes, that she is," I said as we smiled, and nodded at each other in a male bonding, wink, wink, sort-of-way. I liked the old-guy. He had a decent demeanour, something sadly lacking around me these days.

As we pulled in front of the Jeep, Andy waved his arm with a grand gesture saying, "That is some big city gal-pal you have for a girlfriend son."

"Oh yeah, Andy she is uptown all right, but she is not my girlfriend. I just met her today," I proclaimed lifting the Jeep's hood.

We had the engine purring in no time. I got out my wallet and asked, "How much do I owe you?"

"Aw, five bucks will cover it," he said patting me on the back, "everyone needs a break now and then. You come on back to visit sometime. I like those UBC sticky cinnamon buns."

I drove away thinking of Annie. Later that night, the big debate between me, myself, and I, was whether or not to go to the party at Annie's "friend's" house. My dad died eleven years ago, and I still miss him more than I can say. Dad would often say, "Peter, trouble often comes on its own. The question is: Do you need to seek it out?"

Of course, I had an inkling that Annie was the kind of trouble dad warned me to try and avoid. But, hey, on the other hand, life is for living. This is not a dress rehearsal. This is it; the moment is now. Trite, trite, trite, trivial too.

It was a hot early September evening and there I was driving down South West Marine Drive looking at the piece of paper Annie had scribbled the address. Nice homes along the road with a great ocean view. Of course, stands to reason, you could not see the best mansions because tall cedar trees and laurel hedges hide them from view.

The party was easy enough to find. All I had to do was follow the music. They had a bandstand setup by the swimming pool. People were drinking, dancing, and bopping to the max. Annie was nowhere to be seen, so I wandered around the place, while checking out life in the bourgeoisie's ghetto. Nice fountains, flower gardens, and the masonry were impressive, too. But the sculptures were amazing. I had no idea how much that kind of art was worth, probably a lot.

Dad did red and yellow cedar sculptures. After his heart attack he left the practice of law trading statutes for carved statues. At first I thought it was a dumb idea, but it worked out okay for dad. In fact towards the end he was actually earning some good coin from the work.

I sauntered inside the house. There were a lot of people milling about discussing the meaning of life, politics, and current events. Out of the corner of my eye I caught sight of Annie jawing it up in what could only be considered "The Library." She was explaining the inequities in the present system of taxation and why reform is necessary. The guys seemed more interested in their pints of draught beer. Whatever, eh, it is a party.

"Hey Mack," Annie hollered as she spotted me leaning against the door frame, "glad you could make it. I want to introduce you to the MDEC aka Marine Drive Economics Club."

Turns out, the guys were actually all right. They were old friends from Annie's undergraduate days. Russell, the guy Annie was debating most vigorously, was also in law school. More specifically, our class, but I didn't recognize him. Russell was almost arrogant with me. However, it was Annie he showered with scorn and sarcasm.

"Miss Jarman, your ignorance of taxation is only exceeded by a misplaced liberal idealism for dismantling some supposed class structure imposed by the bourgeoisie," Russell didactically demonstrated to Annie and the rest of the MDEC.

"Russell, *YOU* continue to prove, again, quite simply, that you are a buffoon of the first order," Annie declared with desperation. "Macko, as a former denizen of central Canada, what do you think?"

"First of all, I'm from Vancouver Island," I said, correcting Annie, "and, second, I think the middle class is heavily taxed because there are so many of them. The idea of taxing the hell out of the rich has always been popular. The problem is capital gains are either hidden or under reported. Moreover, rich people are fewer in numbers. There are so many middle class wage earners, who can't hide income, or dodge with shelters, support the system. The current government and previous just hand out large corporate tax cuts cuz that is how it works."

Annie rolled her eyes and began to speak when the band kicked in with some loud rock and roll. Finally, thankfully, Annie was drowned-out.

Turns out the MDEC guys were basically okay, except Russell. He was too weird for words. I quaffed the rest of my beer and tried to excuse myself saying, "Well, thanks for the brew Annie. I have an early morning class tomorrow, so I better hit the road."

"Nonsense," she said clutching my arm and leading me out towards the pool, "we haven't danced yet!"

Annie just does not take no for an answer. You can't argue with her. It was no use anyway. So, there I was doing some sort of a version of a jive. "Great band," I yelled putting Annie through another spin cycle, "who owns this place and what do they do?"

"It is Russell's parents place. They are off on their yacht. Old money, you know. They made zillions in forestry. When they are away, Russell throws the greatest parties. Are you having fun Mack-man?"

"Oh yeah, this is great," I hollered back over the music, "but I really should make an exit. Morning comes early."

"Mack, you loser, lighten-up, have some fun. Morning is more than a time zone away."

So, what the hay, I decided to let go and party hearty. It was great. I think I had a good time. But oh man was my neck sore when I woke to find myself sleeping, beer in hand, in a deck chair by the pool with the sun shining in my eyes. There were a few people around in various states of consciousness and lots of party debris scattered around. However, there was no sign of Annie anywhere. I looked at my watch, remembered my morning class, and had a partial panic attack, all in a simultaneous milli-second.

Tiptoeing I tried to quietly slip into Professor Sheppard's class. Of course, wouldn't you know it, I tripped over Russell's feet, dropped a book, and everyone turned around to gawk. And with a wide toothpaste smile, there was Annie.

"Delighted you could join us this morning Mr. Mackintosh," said Professor Sheppard from the front of the room, "sorry, we started without you."

Slinking into my seat, I felt like death, or close to it. How did Annie get here so early? How can she look so good? And geez did she look good. I felt like tepid trash. Annie looked fresh and perky in ironed creased clothes. I was still in my party apparel. Wish I had showered and shaved.

After class finally ended, I made my way through the coffee line-up. Annie jostled and jumped in front of me. "Hey party animal, nice to see you have regained consciousness. Man, once you passed out last night, that was it, lights out and curtains drawn. Don't think you should have got into to the tequila shooters. Actually, I don't think you should have hit the flaming brandy snifters either. Have you never heard: Don't mix grains and grapes?"

"Annie, Annie, timeout eh," I thought she would never stop with the recapitalization. Doesn't she need to come up for air?

"What, you having a little hangover trouble this morning Mr. Mackintosh?" she asked ruffling my hair. I hate having my hair ruffled, but I could muster a small smile. I was thinking to myself, and speaking under my breath, "Annie, you are an obnoxious little so-and-so."

After a while Annie and I became best friends. Law school sort of bonded us in an uncanny way. After we had been beaten-up by exams and the Socratic curriculum, we became sorta soul mates. We looked at life in a similar way. Except, it was all just a joke to Annie, and believe me law school had a lot of jokers, a lot of material and characters to observe with all these people thrown together in a competitive fervour. So many of these people walked around thinking one day they would be Prime Minister or a Supreme Court Judge. Frightening thing was it could happen. Oh yeah, some of these law students would likely hold quite likely the reins of power.

I was never that ambitious. Annie, on the other hand, represents the epitome of ambition.

II.

ANNIE JARMAN

Annie Lynne Jarman was born on a sunny Chinook morning in Calgary, Alberta. She came into the world kicking and screaming and has lived every day pretty much the same way since she started: Loud, brash, and deliberate.

Annie's proud father, Mr. Robert P. Jarman worked as an oil executive. He met the elegant and charming Barbara Joyce Holden while stationed in Houston, Texas for a five-year stint. Not quite love at first sight. Miss Holden was working in a competitive oil marketing division and that alone caused some friction towards the always-aggressive Robert Putman Jarman's style. Moreover, Barbara's parents did not approve of the relationship. It was not just the fact that Jarman was a Canadian. Nor the fact that Jarman was a corporate lawyer, although neither stood as assets. It was Jarman's hyperactivity and incessant verbal barrage of opinions and style that grated Barbara's parents. They would have preferred their daughter marry a southern gentleman, or at least a gentleman.

Worst was when R P Jarman married Barbara J Holden and they moved to the top of the hemisphere. The Holdens had heard of Canada, but they never thought one of their children would leave Texas for less than an exotic land. However, grandchildren cushioned the conundrum of Canadian citizenship. Especially Annie, she was everyone's favourite.

As a young child, Annie and her younger brother Jedd would spend summers visiting Texas along with their mother. JP was too busy for Texas. Except for the period of time when he had been promoted to Vice President of Research and Development and stationed for *another* five year stint in Houston.

Those were Annie's Junior High years. Those were the years that Annie blossomed from a gangly girl to a confident accomplished young scholar. Annie was a voracious reader. Her writing and debating skills began to flourish. Athletically, she took on track and field with a zeal only exceeded by her passion for politics.

As President of her class, Annie organized a protest picket line to point out problems with exploitation of migrant workers in the school cafeteria. Immigration officials actually raided the lunchroom arresting workers without correct document cards. Annie and her friends were detained and later released into the custody of their respective parents. Seems lying down in front of the school's driveway did not go over well with authorities.

In the summer months Houston is *unbearably hot.* Everything and everywhere is air-conditioned. To combat the heat, noise, and pollution in the city the Jarman's bought a beach house in Cayucos, California. Both Galveston and Corpus Christi, Texas were a close second and third runner-up - Mrs. Jarman's older brother and younger sister have summer homes in each locale, respectively. And although extended family barbecues and a summer soirees with relatives and life-long friends has always been a priority, the moment she set eyes on the beach house in Cayucos, Mrs. J was in love with the sprawling yellow rancher that sat on the edge of a fifteen foot drop off to the beach. It was a mid-bank waterfront home. The old place was a bit rundown, but had a view of the ocean that was uncompromising. Annie was less than enamoured with the place, and Jedd balked at the idea. But, Jedd balked at most ideas that involve a change of residence for any length of time.

Cayucos is a coastal jewel of a beach community lying halfway between Los Angeles and San Francisco. What could be better for a business commuter? R P Jarman was able to cram family-life, recreation, and a business connection afloat in his study at the rancher. Barbara Joyce worked on watercolour paintings of the community. Jedd and Annie learned how to surf, and sea kayaking was a popular pastime.

Annie and her mother took frequent field trips throughout the coastal community. They were often sketching and painting. Art was their bonding time. The community had a lot of variety to offer. Cayucos is bordered by the Pacific Ocean with spectacular headlands and beaches on the one side. The rugged Santa Lucia Mountains ringed the other side. Spectacular sun rises and sunsets competed with each other. Both provided colours for a young woman and her mother to aspire justice in duplicating.

Morro Rock stands in the middle of Morro Bay, just south of Cayucos and north of the college town of San Luis Obispo where Cal Poly University sends cadres of students to the beach to admire the 576-foot high granite rock known as the "Gibraltar of the Pacific." It was Annie's favourite place to picnic and paint sunsets. The late afternoon's strong sunshine rolled into early evening sunsets which in turn became late summer night's where the sky was dotted with stars and planets. Mrs. Jarman and Annie loved to lie on their blankets in the sand searching the sky for shooting stars to wish upon. As an adult Annie would remember this as one of the happiest times in her life. It was simple and life was easy.

"Mama, do you think there is life beyond our known universe," Annie asked, "you know Extra Terrestrials and all that sort of stuff."

"I do not know Annie," her mother replied with a smile, "I think we must always keep an open mind to the things scientists do not have answers."

"That is for sure, science has some way to go as far as I am concerned, but you have got to have faith, I guess."

Smiling and nodding her heard, Mrs. J replied, "Yes, you have got to have some faith, and hope, too.

Annie kept an open mind. She questioned everyone and everything. She also learned some semblance of sensitivity from her mother's influence. These personality traits served Annie well while growing into an opinionated, strong, but also a semi-sensitive woman.

III.

PARISIAN PREBENDARIES

After law school Annie and I went our separate ways. Life rolls on one-way or another. Annie moved to Montreal. She got married, divorced, remarried and divorced again. Annie just couldn't seem to get it right, but she sure strived to believe in marriage as a social institution. Catholics are funny that way, eh?

We tried to keep in touch for a while. But, you know, time turns and twists along, where one thing leads to another, days turn to weeks, weeks, to months, and months to years. The next thing you know too many years have flown by. I was sitting at my desk shuffling files when Annie telephoned out of the blue from Paris.

"Bonjour Peter," said a familiar voice from so many chapters ago, "how is the practice of law proceeding?"

"Hey, Annie Jarman," I replied with nothing but surprise and a happy tone of voice, "is that really you?" Then I laughed and asked, "What is your surname now, Tremblay, Julson or Krasnov or are you back to Jarman?"

"Yes," she chortled with an all too familiar laugh that I remembered from way back when life was at a different age and stage, "I've gone back to my maiden name."

"Oh please, I've never thought of you as a 'maiden' Annie," I started to break out laughing like so many times as we use to all those law school years ago. Annie could always crack me up. She was so funny. She has always had a twisted sense of humour. I liked it and, indeed, identified with her style.

Time travels by and we march along doing our things. You win some, lose some, and that is how it goes. Annie's last phone call to me was after her second divorce. She had felt bad when her first marriage failed, and felt worse when her second marriage detonated and blew-up in her face. Her husband had been cheating on her. He kept saying he would stop cheating, but never did. Annie finally left after all the lies just became too much to bear anymore.

Medically speaking, from what I can deduce, guess Annie was depressed and a bit manic the last time we spoke. She was telling me that she was having "serious problems." When I inquired what was going on she explained that she was simply having problems "being serious." She had been through the wringer so many times she was having problems being serious about pedestrian problems that use to burn up her energy. Wardrobe issues were not as important anymore. It was hard for me to follow her conversation. That did not really bother me. Historically, I always had trouble following Annie's verbal discourse. Making sense just was something she did not always sustain. But, she was a brilliant and creative thinker.

"So kay-passa Annie," I asked continuing our old inside joke that only we thought was funny, "what's happening in Paris?"

"Nothing," she replied, "that is why I am coming back to Vancouver next week. I have a business opportunity to explore. Can you do lunch, dinner, or 'something' on Thursday?" she asked.

Another old line, which she used so many times before, that was way back when. She was probably my best friend while we whiled our way through law school. "Of course," I cautioned, "you need to know the Hong Kong Kitchen burned down a few years ago. Only to be replaced by a yuppie bagel joint. But, hey, there is always Bishops on Fourth."

"Fine, Peter, whatever. You look after it. I'll call when I get in."

That was it, she hung up and I was left shaking my head with the telephone in my hand. Annie was coming back to Vancouver. Wow, weird, eh. What would this bring? I wondered.

The YVR (Vancouver International Airport) located on Sea Island in between the City of Vancouver and the bedroom burb of Richmond, is always "under construction." As a teenager I would travel semi-regularly from Cape Lazo on Vancouver Island to visit my mother in New York City. The first few trips between Cape Lazo and NYC were not what I wanted to do. My mother and father forced me to sojourn. After dad died I almost grew to enjoy my trips to NYC, but I always hated the Vancouver International Airport. Not just because I always had a "lay-over" but the lame and expensive food, long lineups, and the fact that the place was never the same from one time to another. They were always renovating. I could never find my way around. Worst was when you landed and had to walk from a time zone away to customs. And I always choose the slowest line with the crankiest custom agent that is mid-shift and disdainful. You know the type, eh.

Annie's plane was late. I was apprehensive. The place was crowded. People kept bashing into me. And I was getting marginally anxious. I didn't really know why. It was Annie for goodness sake. I had picked her up at the airport too many times before in the old daze. But this time I was apprehensive. In my mind I was reviewing the sequencing but for the life of me I could not remember exactly when and where I last saw Annie.

Once, after law school, I saw Annie and her 'new' husband in Montreal. They lived in a posh mansion in the Mount Royal district. They presented well. You know, fine homes, nice cars, and the lot. Somehow, I knew that Annie and Alexandre would not last the long run. Sure, they presented well, but they just did not seem like a good "fit." I did not know exactly what kind of man would fit Annie, but I knew it wasn't Alexandre. Sure enough, when Annie learned of his infidelity, she left.

Next, Annie married a tennis player, Michel Tremblay. They travelled the world using Paris as a home base. A couple of years ago we met in Los Angeles while I was visiting my Stepsister, Veronica, and Mich (he hated it when I called him Mich) was playing in a tournament. Annie was in a mood when we met at Newport Beach. We didn't have much time together as she had to get back to see a tennis match and I had to arrive "on time" to Ronnie's party. And that was that, a sort of thing.

The next time I saw Annie was during my European vacation - three girlfriends ago. Jacqueline was her first name. Funny how I had strings of J's: Jacqueline, Judy, Dr Jaswali, and Ms. Annie J. But, of course, Annie didn't really count because we were only good friends. Nonetheless, she has a J with the Jarman surname. There was a time when I would spend too much time with her -way back when. So it counts for something, I guess.

We met in a pleasant Paris cafe. Annie had divorced Mich and was doing a rare solo stint. I still smile at the thought. Annie was never solo for long, always monogamous, but a serial dater. Annie always had suitors, many, many suitors.

I loved Paris. Expensive, but nice, I hadn't been there for years. And because I knew Annie was there, Paris was put on the European itinerary. She was a great tour guide, too. Annie knew how to work the town, where to go and how to get there.

Annie was her old radiant self in the cafe. With a wide sweeping gesture, Annie lectured how "Paris is portioned and divided into twenty arrondissements that pinwheel in a clockwise fashion outward from the Louvre at the centre of the city. Each of the respective arrondissements, or "es," is like their own separate distinctive principality. Each has its own mayor with a municipal make-up. So you see, half of the arrondissements are on the Right Bank of the Seine River and the other halves are on the Left Bank."

Nodding and smiling throughout her spiel, I remembered how Annie spoke. Her passion, and, of course, how I could never ever get a word in edgewise. Then, while Annie was pulling in a breath I asked, "Where are we now?"

"Oh, yes, this is 'restaurant row', and if you look on the map here," pointing to nowhere I could actually encode and decipher, Annie continued. "We are now at 5e which is known as rue de la Huchette."

"Uh huh," was my murmur, "and tonight?" I queried, full knowing another spiel was en route.

"Thank you for reminding me," Annie began to tell me about the party in the Latin Quarter. "And, you know Peter, the Latin Quarter has nothing to do with your experiences in Mexico. It comes from Roman architectural influences."

Leaning forward and clasping her hands in an attempt to get her to slow down and take a time-out, I said, "Thanks AJ, I've got it."

Without missing a beat, Annie replied, "Great, pick you up at seven. Or nineteen hundred, if you still prefer the twenty-four hour military clock."

Annie had graciously offered me a room to stay in at her apartment, but she and Michel had just spilt. I did not think it wise to be there. Even though Annie and I were old friends with no romantic ties, I did not want to offer any fodder to Mich and their residual divorce dance steps. Besides, we both needed space and separate bathrooms.

Of course, needless to say, Annie booked me into an excellent room at Hotel Luxembourg at rue de Vaugirard. Fourteen-foot ceilings, king-size bed, big bathroom, and a lovely view of the courtyard garden, it was a great place to stay, very exquisite.

After divorcing Mich, Annie got involved in the art business. She seemed to be doing well. But, hey, what do I know about the art business? Nonetheless, she seemed happy the last time I saw her. I just couldn't remember when that was. I knew Paris wasn't the last time I saw Annie. It may have been back a few years or so ago when she breezed in and out of Vancouver. Or it may have been when I was visiting my mother in NYC. Don't know, just can't remember the date or episode. Time flies too fast.

Shuffling my feet on the spot while standing at the arrival area, I wondered how Annie would look now. Whether the last number of years had been kind, or had she aged hard? Would she recognize me with my salt and pepper hair and four extra kilograms of weight, which came with aging? At least, unlike Russell, I hadn't gone bald, not that there is anything wrong with baldness, of course.

So there I was, spacing out of the ozone. Watching people meeting loved ones, baggage bashing down the carousel and little kids crying from travel woes, when all of a sudden, there she was: Annie Jarman the one and only in person, strolling straight towards me.

Holding out her arms for an impending embrace, I heard a familiar voice from way-back- when say, "Well, well, well, look at you, Mr. Peter Mackintosh, you've grownup." With European pecks on each cheek and a big firm hug, that was it, Annie was back. And it was great to see her and all her glory. She looked terrific.

Too bad this rendezvous would not last long and Annie would be gone, again. Just like that. She left a note stuffed below my door, "Dear Peter, I have to leave town tonight. Got to get myself together. Talk soon, love Annie."

IV.

LETTERS TO ANNIE

Dear Annie,

Your mother gave me this address. Barbara J always had a soft spot for me, as you know. So, how are you doing? Where did the time go? Time has always been an issue; I have never really understood the construct. I say construct because people invented the idea of time. It has always been too abstract for me; can't see it, can't touch it, sometimes try and kill it, and sometimes never have enough time.

Time is only a semi-sophisticated time. It isn't real, and I don't know how it feels. It's just a bit this side of too abstract anyways, eh. Remember, James Taylor wrote a song called "*The Secret of Life*" is enjoying the passage of time. Do you also remember playing JT, Zeppelin, and Rolling Stones cassettes while we were cranking out law school memos, factums, and papers? You cannot even buy a cassette in this digital age. Russell thinks he can tell the difference between digital and analog. He is like that, as you all too well know.

Remember when I told you my father did not have enough time. He died from a heart attack at age fifty-two. Nice obituaries were written. They say dad died at middle age. What is middle age? When will we be middle-aged? I have always stuck with Mark Twain's notion that "middle-age people are always ten years older than me."

I did not have enough time with dad. I still miss him more than I can tell you. Everyone said time would heal the pain. They were wrong. I deal with it better these days, but I still have the three in the morning sessions where I stare out the window, wondering. I always envied how you could rack-out for ten hours, IN A ROW! It would have been nice to be a sleeper, but I have always been in a hurry, some things always needed attention. Deadlines and things that needed to be dealt with and done always seemed a time stealing priority.

As a kid at Cape Lazo, I remember looking at the calendar dad had tacked to the wall by the refrigerator. Time troubled me then. I would turn the pages and count out six months or so until my birthday saying, "I'll never make it, too much time to go." Now time goes too fast where birthdays turn up with surprise parties and people planting kisses and shaking my hand too loosely. I hate surprise parties.

I miss you more than I can scratch out on this piece of paper. I wish we had more time together. I am sorry things did not work out here in Vancouver. I am sorry you had to leave. I wish you could have stayed longer. It was fun-passing time with you, again. When can I come and visit? You said I could come see you when things settled. Have things settled? I would love to see you.

HUGS

Love Peter

Dear Annie,

Thank you for the post card from Bali. The hotel looks great. I hope you are having a good time. I have tried to call you on the telephone, but you seem hard to get a hold of.

Sorry things didn't ever settle back in Paris. I would have enjoyed visiting you. I remember what a great time we had partying in the Latin Quarter. That was such a blast, sort of reminded me of the old party daze with the Marine Drive Economics Club. Don't you sometimes wonder where the old gang went? I have lost touch with pretty well everyone, except Russell. Of course, we still take the eight-kilometer run along James Cunningham's seawall in Stanley Park on Sunday mornings. It is still Russell's main religion. He will never change. He has always been so competitive, driven, and striving to be the best. Remember the gold medal thing at law school. It is still a big deal for Russell. I learned to shake things off years ago. Recalcitrant, yes, that is my ambition.

So Annie, what about you? What are you doing? When can I come and see you? When are you going to return? Hey, how about returning my phone calls, for starters, eh.

I wish I knew what was going on in your bubble. Where are you orbiting? Tell me what is going on. You know: Kay Passé! Throw me a bone!

Love Peter

Dear Annie,

Thank you for the post card from Athens. The Acropolis looks a bit Disney-like. How long are you going to stay in Greece?

Do you remember that spring when we were in Greece Island hopping? I remember the Isle of Rhodes when you asked for a turn driving the rented Vespa. I thought you knew what you were doing. The last thing I expected was for you to pop the clutch and pull a wheelie. Of course, the last thing you expected was for the Vespa to flip on top of us. I liked the hospital in Lindos. Made some new friends, got a few stitches. You know regular tourist stuff.

Russell is getting married, again. He asked me to be the best man. I am looking forward to roasting him in a toast. Sure would be great if you could attend. It is going to be a lavish affair at the Point Grey Golf Club. Janice seems nice. I am sure Russell as a fiancée is a bit of a stretch. But, hey, she seems to love him. Whoa-wee scary spice, eh. I still run into Carol, Russell's first wife, up at the UBC pool when I swim. I am trying to do more cross training to save stress on my knees from pavement pounding running.

Give me a call. I would love to hear from you. See if you can make it to Russell's wedding. He would love to see you, too. It would be like the old daze. Good times.

Love Peter

Dear Annie,

Russell's wedding went well. Wish you could have been there. I got a bit too drunk and woke-up in West Van. You know the after party-after party. I didn't do anything too stupid, but you know how hard it is for me to know when to draw-the-line, quit while I am ahead, and all that sort of stuff. It's not easy.

At the pre-wedding dinner party we played the "best memory/worst memory game" with Russell, Janice, and her friend, Diana, aka my blind date, so to speak. For me, some of these things are like opening a can of worms where the lid is best left in place.

Remember my old adage: Once you squeeze the toothpaste out, it is hard to get it back in the tube. Oh yeah, some things are best compartmentalized.

On the other hand, dealing with memories is also the "stuff of life." My best memory of my father was sailing Desolation Sound. My worst memory was sailing Desolation Sound where he had a fatal heart attack.

My best memory of you was the first day we met in the parking lot at UBC. You were nuts from the start. My worst memory was the day you left me holding a terse note saying you had to get away for a while. And it was "for-the-best," and I would understand in time.

Well, time has gone by and I still don't understand. Moreover, the "for-the-best" business placates for a while but undersells at the end of the day. Sorry things have turned out this way. Remember, on the list of people pressuring you; please place my name three below the last line. It's not my style or my role to pressure you. Annie, I am your FRIEND.

Peter

V.

PYGMY DREAMS

Mental illness is a silent stalker. Sneaks up and sucker punches the wind from your lungs. Mental illness douses the dignity and decency in dealing with life. Mental illness strikes without any discrimination at all. Although we like to think it happens to others, rich people, poor people, successful people, educated people; young and old can be debilitated and destroyed. Some cultures and ethnic groups pretend it doesn't happen to their people. They are lying, it does. There is no exemption clause for special people or religious leaders or pusillanimous political pundits who usually profit from position.

Mental illness happens. There is the constant search for a cure, a pill, or a panacea. A differential diagnosis is difficult, according to the experts. Annie met too many experts. Experts gave her blood workups, Positron Emission Topography (PET) scans, Magnetic Resonance Imaging (MRI), genetic predisposition tests, neuroleptic drug trials, Minnesota Multiphasic Personality Inventory, Rorschach blots, Bender Visual-Motor Gestalt, and the Luria-Nebrasba Neuropsychological Battery.

Of all the many, many doctors Annie dealt with, she liked Dr. Quan at the University British Columbia Hospital's Mood Disorder Clinic. He seemed honest, straightforward and told the truth without sugarcoating, condescending, or confabulating. Indeed, he was helpful. Dr. Quan explained that although Annie thought she was hearing intrusive voices, she was not. There were no voices. There are no ghosts or goblins. Rather, Annie could hear the blood gushing and rushing around the temporal lobes of her brain. She misinterpreted those stimuli as voices. The voices were not real.

Insidious schizophrenia, as Dr. Quan explained, can have a gradual onset of symptoms. Sometimes family members, or even the person themselves, may not notice that anything is wrong for a period of time until there is an acute crisis episode of schizophrenia. Generally, an acute episode is usually short and intense, and involves auditory or visual hallucinations, delusions, thought disorders, and an altered sense of self.

For Annie, the bad news was, as she listened intently to Dr. Quan, all of the above tennis balls were bouncing around all over the place in her court, had been for a while. She had been swinging her racquet at as many of them as she could. It's just that they kept coming. Too many, too fast, and the ones she thought would fall long were short. The ones she thought would be wide were inside. Then they would blur. Lose score and not know where to stand. Which side was which and it is so confusing.

Actually, Annie had sort of known for a while things were not working out well. And that is why she moved back to Vancouver with the hope of finding peace and a place of familiarity to sort it out. Get her feet back on solid ground. When she was in France, she was depressed. Then she divorced. Then she was depressed and delusional. Maybe she had been delusional for a while. Things that were supposed to make sense didn't. People, who she thought understood her, didn't. Nothing was right. Everything was wrong and slowly sliding past worse into worst. Bad was a while a go. She missed the bad times, now that things were worse.

Although Annie had driven to the UBC Hospital, she stumbled out into a typical Vancouver drizzle and began slowly walking home. It wasn't until she turned north at the end of Chancellor Boulevard onto Blanca that she remembered leaving her car parked in B-lot. Later, tomorrow, or whenever, the car would be fine. Annie never paid attention to UBC parking regulations before, why start now? Besides, she enjoyed walking in the rain. By the time she reached Locarno Beach the sky was dark and the rain picked up the pace. It felt good to have her legs moving and mind drifting.

Annie remembered how people use to speak of the 'wet coast' and how some mornings you could make the room darker simply by opening the curtains. The lack of light outside sucked the inside light out. Prairie people often come to Vancouver and suffer claustrophobia in the winter because the low cloud ceiling locked in by the north Shore Mountains. Oh, her dear friend Peter. What will she do with him? He wouldn't be able to get his head around this whole thing, she knew that much for sure. Still, she thought to call and explain. At a phone box by Jericho Beach, Annie dialed his number only to get the voice mail. No, not this time Peter, she couldn't leave a message. What would she say anyway? Hanging-up the receiver, Annie began crying, softly at first, then the full shaking torrent of tears inside the phone box and outside, too. This was not going to be one of those solace sonnets where Peter or anyone could say anything to make it seem 'better'.

After gaining some semblance of composure, Annie started walking again, slowly at first, and then picking up the pace to a jogging run down Point Grey Road, through Tatlow Park and up to her apartment at 5th and Bayswater. She took off all her wet togs and placed them in a heap by the doorway, showered at length, drank herbal tea, and slept for twelve hours. Dr. Quan had warned her that the new meds might "interact" with circadian rhythms, sleep patterns and dreams may be affected, too.

No kidding, eh, Dr. Quan. Annie had always been a lucid dreamer, but now images were even more vivid. Annie dreamed of her childhood, running along the beach in Cayucos with her brother Jedd. These days Jedd had his own problems to deal with. While working on his PhD, with an attempt to win the Nobel Prize for science -- Jedd worked "all the time" - he neglected to pay adequate attention to his wife; someone else did. Thus, the marriage dissolved, or it detonated, if you will imagine Jedd as the last-one-to-know rage.

Annie's dreams were wild and weird, too many things going on in her head. Insidious schizophrenia and temporal lobe blood flow notwithstanding, Annie's brain bounced all over the sleep cycle. Peter, the former amateur anthropologist, and now 'gentleman lawyer' pontificating on pygmy's perceptions on dreams, "A number of cardiac researchers, psychologists and physiologists have hypothesized that some people die in their sleep as a result of a powerful dream experience," Peter spoke in lecture mode. "The pygmies knew this a long time ago. They cut holes in the roof of huts in order to let the spirit wander at night. If a pygmy was hunting in his sleep and could not return to the hut from a dreaming hunt, he would die. Similarly, if a pygmy died while hunting in dream land, he would also die in day life." Peter, winding-up, continued saying, "Therefore, in western society we may infer deaths while sleeping may also be attributed to one's dream experience."

Religion, oh yeah, Annie had some thoughts on religion. As a child, religion was frightening, as an adult, confusing, and as a schizophrenic, even more confusing. Russell was religious, her father, religious. Peter pushed a cross-cultural anthropological perspective on religious practices around the world. "The pygmies' gods were the sun and river. Which, of course, is logically consistent considering both sustain pygmy life? And when you consider the audacity of western missionaries telling the pygmies their gods were wrong and the *real god* was not in the river or sun. No wonder the pygmies killed them."

Annie was set in her ways, too. Still, Peter's point about every, and I mean every, culture on the planet practices some form of religion. Annie went out with a Buddhist for a while, or maybe he was a Sikh. What was his name?

Thought disorders. Dr. Quan had explained some of Annie's behaviour as "delusional." This was not new news; however, it seemed more of a problem with a professional endorsement. The idea of delusions seemed so icky. "So the thing is my brain is processing information incorrectly and my thoughts are disordered. Is that what you are saying?" Annie asked with her best lawyer-like staccato style cross-examine voice.

"Yes," Dr. Quan replied, "your thoughts are disordered. You are misinterpreting both auditory and visual information and this deludes you into a behavioural response not in keeping with normal information processing. We are hoping the medication will mitigate these symptoms you are experiencing."

"I am not paranoid," Annie explained, "if anything, I am positively *pronoid*. Well, at least I was before all this confusion."

You see paranoid people are always looking over their shoulder thinking people are saying and thinking unfavourable things about them. Pronoid people, on the other hand, sally forth thinking everyone likes them, everything they touch turns to gold, and the only people who fail are those that do not try. Half empty or half full, it is perceptual.

Nonverbal visual cues, sure, she misunderstood the man who bumped beside her in the elevator. It was a crowded elevator, but nonetheless he did not need to touch her. Did he? It seemed sexually untoward.

"I don't know, guess I am mental," Annie said softly shaking her head. "Having sex with Peter was mental. I mean really mental! One thing led to another or something like that, or maybe nothing like that. I don't know. Dom Perignon did it."

Annie thought about it, makes sense, but still a mental-like thing to do. Not that there had always been a lot of sexual tension brewing, but maybe there was. "Peter and I were almost like brother and sister. Oh shit, that makes it worse: incest. Or something that should not have happened. But, oh yeah, it did." Annie sighed softly.

"People don't plan to fail, they fail to plan. Peter the planner certainly did not have an agenda; he simply wanted to celebrate his birthday with me. I had mostly forgotten it but not completely as I had just placed the day on the top shelf of the horizon and it appeared too suddenly."

"The whole sexual dance has a rhythm I have never kept pace gracefully. Sure, I had always thought Peter as attractive. But, we were friends. Good friends. Although, after we had a couple of *splashes* of champagne, we became friendlier. It started with the accidental bumping into one another. The lingering touch of the hand, then it was the kiss. The first was short and sweet. The second, third, and fourth were passionate. It felt good. It was a release. It was Peter, naked, tender, and full of hormones hoping to escape!"

Dr. Quan nodded, "What happened next?"

"Morning came, and went. We stayed in bed until three in the afternoon. We must have made love a dozen times. It was great. That is, as long as I *stayed in the moment*."

But the moment was just the same old thing, a moment. Not that long term planning was all that enticing given the parameters.

VI.

WHISTLER MOUNTAIN

My father, Jason Martin Mackintosh, died while we were on a sailing trip shooting the tide's rapids in dinghies at a place called Squirrel Cove in Desolation Sound off Vancouver Island. I remember it as though it was yesterday. I have played and replayed the image of his heart attack too many times. Everyone always said, "I would get over it. Time would heal the pain. And life goes on."

Well, truth is, I never got over my dad's death, and time has never healed the wound. I just live with it, everyday. You actually do not get over a loved one's departure; you live with it. Same thing with Annie's sudden departure, I live with it, too. I don't know why she left, where she is or what she is doing now.

When I first met Russell, I did not like him much. He was rich, urbane, erudite, and awfully arrogant. Some years have since passed since law school and Russell is still rich, urbane, and awfully arrogant. Nowadays though, he is my best friend. It took too long to get to know him. But, once you get over his demeanour and disposition, he is okay, and certainly a good friend. Russell has known Annie longer than I have, but confesses to saying, "Nobody really knows anyone anyways."

Of course, even at the best of times, it was hard for me to take Russell seriously. He is a rich goofball. I had tried to explain the whole Annie thing, but he was sitting across from me wearing a t-shirt that reads: "If it has Tits or Wheels, Count on Problems!" He had just returned from a Mexican sojourn with a tan and tacky souvenirs. His divorce to second wife, Janice was well in the works. We were spending time at their Whistler condo before the divorce property settlement determined who gets which assets. I liked Janice. I liked their Whistler condo, too.

Although Russell's family has a nice modest mansion overlooking the golf course at Whistler, but, with Janice's urging, as newly weds, they bought their own condo under the auspices of a *good investment.* Also, a vernacular understanding that the space was a good idea to keep separated from family functions and affairs. Russell was good at compartmentalization. His parents had been early Whistler patrons buying property in the 1970s, developing the village, and promoting skiing in the valley. Russell says that he recalls learning to walk and immediately thereafter they placed boards on his feet. He learned to ski at a young age.

I loved going to Whistler; winter, spring, summer or fall, it was always a good call. In some ways Whistler reminded me of Cape Lazo where I spent my teenage years. The ski resort was first developed back in the late sixties and early seventies. Whistler Mountain was named for the whistling call of the Western Hoary Marmot. This furry little inhabitant of the alpine meadows was once on the brink of extinction, but has bounced back and has had increasing numbers in recent years.

I was always a hanger-on with Russell at Whistler. When we first started skiing together, Whistler was the main domain for skiers. Blackcomb Mountain opened some years later and all the snowboarders flocked to those boarder friendly slopes. Now with the increasing boom and popularity of snow boards they are almost starting to dominate both mountains.

We were sitting on the deck of Russell's condo drinking beer when I said, "Hey, do you remember the movie Tootsie?"

Shaking his head and pulling a swig, Russell coughed out a "No."

"C'mon man we watched the DVD at the MDEC film festival last year. Tootsie is a classic. Remember the part when Dustin Hoffman reveals on camera in his soap opera character that he was not a woman, but really a man. Oh, and Jessica Lang felt so betrayed. She loved Dorothy. Soon as the scene was over Jessica stood up, slugged Dustin (Dorothy) in the stomach, and stomped off the set. Few days later, while drinking some beers with Jessica's father, Dustin (Dorothy) realizes the toothpaste was squeezed out of the tube and cannot be put back inside. Following fatherly advice Dustin (Dorothy) met with Jessica and tried to explain. He never wanted anyone to get hurt, especially Jessica. Then when Jessica shrugs and says she misses Dorothy. Dustin explains that Dorothy is right here beside her. The best line was when he tells her that he was a better man as a woman with Jessica than he ever was as a man with a woman. Russell, get it?"

Struggling to follow and growing impatient with what was my point, Russell popped open a fresh beer, saying, "Yes, Peter, classic film, but what is the moral of this story? Do you have a thesis here?"

"Yes, here's the point, when Dustin (Dorothy) contorts his face and explains to Jessica – *the hard part is over! We have already gotten to know each other. We are best friends.*"

Shaking his head Russell asks, "What colour is the sky in your world? *It's a movie*!"

"Yes, yes, but it's the best friends part that I liked. The hard work was over. And I liked the happy-sappy ending where Jessica turns to the formerly cross-dressing Dustin (Dorothy) and asks to borrow his yellow dress. Then the theme song pipes in with "I have been waiting all my life for someone like you."

Wrist watch glancing and continued head shaking Russell replies, "Dude, you are the weirdest most random thinker I have ever known."

"I miss Annie. We were such good friends. I miss her rants, her riffs, her ridiculous sense of humour, and everything. I really miss her Russ."

Sighing and more head shaking Russell replied with, "Sex ruined it for you. Once you have done the wild thing you are not friends any more. You cannot be friends with someone you had sex with. It is that simple."

"Russ, nothing is simple."

VII.

VICTOR HUGO BOULEVARD

Rapid eye movements (REM) and the other stages of sleep make sense to most people. We get it. The sleep scientists have demonstrated that sleep deprivation is correlated to physical health. That is, simply, if you are deprived of an adequate amount of sleep your physical health suffers. Without an adequate amount of sleep one becomes sluggish, inattentive, and slow to respond to stimuli.

Similarly, dream deprivation is related to mental health. If you are deprived of dreams your mental health is in jeopardy. In the laboratory people would be allowed to sleep, but as soon as the brain wave machine showed a REM pattern they would wake the person to prevent them from dreaming. Those people who were dream deprived became cranky, irritable, and mentally unstable. Some were marginally psychotic.

And then on the other hand there is the whole Freudian conscious and unconscious paradigm. Dream interpretations, the superego, id, and of course libido inter-relationships are interesting, too. What does a Freudian slip mean? What do dreams mean?

I don't know much, but I was definitely in a deep sleep stage or a complicated and complex dream when the telephone's incessant ringing roused me back to reality. I woke up with a startle. It was five in the afternoon in Paris, but it was 3:00 in the morning in Vancouver.

Some time back I had a brief seven-month fling with Jessica Portsman. Sleep was simply sacrosanct for Jessica. Eight to ten hours of uninterrupted sleep was a high priority. It did not matter whether we were sleeping at her Burnaby bungalow on Holdom Street overlooking the Burrard Inlet and Indian Arm or my crowded condo in Kitsilano, the nightly shutdown routine did not vary. First, the evening wash-up, followed with a mug of warm milk, and then doors and windows were secured, all lights off, and all telephones turned off. Yes, Jess insisted all phones off. And actually, she had a point. Who wants to be wakened by a telephone? Besides, the caller could leave a message without disturbing the sleeper with the phone ringing. Nevertheless, I did not miss Jess after we split, she was really high, high maintenance, but I probably should have continued the telephones off nightly ritual practice.

"Hello" I groggily mumbled fumbling with the telephone.

"Bonjour, par le vous Francais?" was the inquiry.

"Oh no, not really," I was born in Montreal, but I am not really French fluent. "Who is this?" I asked.

"One moment Monsieur," the gentleman said,"s'il vous plaît" and then some stupid music, followed by a new voice.

"Hello, is this Pierre Mackintosh?" the new female voice asked. The only person who ever called me Pierre was Carin Barrington from the island, but this was not her voice. "This is Peter Mackintosh speaking, who is calling please?" I was starting to get annoyed, especially so when I glanced at the clock.

Then a faint familiar voice piped in with "Hi Peter, it is Annie. Sorry, I did not know who to call. I had an accident and need your help. Will you come and get me out of here?"

"Yes, sure, of course Annie," I stammered, "where are you?"

"I am in a Paris hospital, I had an accident."

"What kind of accident?" I asked.

"Got too depressed, took too many pills, washed down with red wine. Just screwed-up."

"Are you okay?"

Annie sighed and slowly murmured, "No Peter, I am all messed-up and I need you to come and get me out of here, please. These French laws say I need a family member to sign me out. I told them you are family. So please come and sign me out of here. I need you Peter."

"Yes, Annie, no problem, I will make the arrangements. It is only 3:15 in the morning, but I am on it. Next flight out, I am on it, Annie, next flight out."

It is not that I have a fear of flying or anything like that, I just hate the airport, airplanes, and the taxi-things associated with flying. Packing problems plague me, too. I never know what to leave in or what to take out of the luggage. I inevitably end up lugging more than I would rather, or need. I am not a good traveller, but it is Annic, so I stumbled around and put a bag together.

Now of course none of this is new or endemic to only me. Stories are told about when Ernest Hemingway settled in Paris in 1921. He became part of the expatriate gaggle of Gertrude Stein, F. Scott Fitzgerald, and Ezra Pound. None of them flew to Paris. They cruised over by boat. It was a different world and traveling was slower. Life was likely simpler, too. They did not have to deal with jetlag and cramped leg thrombosis syndrome. Wonder when did I become such a whiner?

It was pouring rain in Vancouver. Got to the airport within the acceptable check-in time to catch the fourteen-hour flight to Paris. I was awfully anxious and fidgeted the whole flight. I tried to sleep because I knew it would be important to have my wits about me. And even though I was already sleep deprived I couldn't sleep. Just kept ruminating and wondering what I would find in Paris.

With broken French and hand gestures I was able to get an airport taxi to take me to the American Hospital of Paris at 63 boulevards Victor Hugo. Location-wise it was a grand place for a hospital. Although I have always hated hospitals, this one was no exception either. I particularly hate the smells, but guess it could be worse, I suppose, but this was not a holiday vacation. Nevertheless, I hoped we would not stay long. The plan was to get in and get out quickly and get back to Vancouver. I promised Annie I would get her home. No problem, I could handle it. Oh Annie, how did things unravel to this point? How did you end up here?

Our immediate problem aside for a moment, the history of the American Hospital of Paris was intriguing. Apparently in September 1909, Mr. Henry White, Ambassador of the USA to France, and Monsieur Gaston Doumergue, the then Minister of Public Education and the future president of the French Republic, inaugurated the new twenty-four bed hospital with its awfully auspicious goal to offer American expatriates access to health care services provided by physicians trained in America.

Nothing is simple. Getting to actually see Annie was no exception, either. Turns out things were a little more complicated than I was expecting. In addition to ingesting a variety of pharmaceutical pills, illicit drugs, and alcohol, Annie had taken a large serrated sharp knife and slit her wrists up pretty badly. That detail had been omitted during the phone call.

After some bureaucratic finagling I was able to gain entry past the main building foyer reception kiosk, where I was escorted through a maze of corridors to the administrative wing and then I was met by a variety of officials. Some spoke English, some spoke French, and the lawyers did double Dutch renditions of the legal options available.

Suicide notes are never well publicized for privacy and practical reasons. A plastic covered copy of Annie's note was presented to me in the hospital administrator's office. I guess they did not want to give me the original in case I reacted badly and ripped it up or something. I was taken back trying to decipher her prose which was in rambling

English and French. Her final instructions at the end of the missive was to whoever found her body to contact Peter Mackintosh at 604-224-0809. And then her instructions to me were to cremate her body and spread the ashes in Cayucos, California, or second choice, Cape Lazo, British Columbia. Her final destination was left to be my decision. "It is your choice, whatever you think best."

Thinking to myself, oh that Annie J, how considerate, eh? Leaving me to decide where to spread her ashes. Like it was something her brother, parents, or various ex-spouses would not feel some sort of vested interest. Moreover, why was she so far overwrought as to be planning ash spreading venues?

They eventually let me in to see Annie in her private isolated stupid white sterile-like hospital room that overlooked the courtyard. "Hi, Annie, how you doing?" I asked with a voice that desperately tried to contain a quiver and squeak. She seemed to not even know who I was. I attributed it to a combination of her self-medications and the hospital's drugs. I started to cry, and I am sure that was less than helpful. But, hey, what the hell was I suppose to do? It was sad. Annie looked bad. This was not what we wanted back in those happy days when life was easier, breezier, and devoid of hospital smells.

She slurred some words in my direction, but I could not decode whether it was French, English, or schizoids gibberish talk that meant nothing anyway. I stayed for a while; Annie went in and out of sleeping and slurring sentences that made no sense to me, or the attending physician, Dr. Michelle LaSalle.

"It is going to take some time. Monsieur Mackintosh, you are going to have to be patient," Dr. LaSalle cautioned with her heavy French accent, but proficient English. "She is heavily sedated in order to give her body a chance to begin recuperation and repairs," as the doctor examined a chart and squinted at a beeping machine that was hooked into Annie's arm.

"How long do you think before she can go back to Canada?" I asked trying to not sound or look completely overwhelmed and exasperated. "She has an excellent primary physician back home that she has been seeing for a while. Dr. Quan has been a big help."

"We will know more soon," she said with a smile, "I have not seen the latest blood and liver response tests. Maybe you can take her home in a few days. But, it is not going to be easy. I hope you have some help medical and mental health help when you leave here. You are going to need more than medicine help to get back on her feet."

I returned her smile, but mine was a bit on the fake and insecure side, "Oh, oui, yes, we do have things all arranged Dr. LaSalle thank you." The truth was I had phoned Russell Webster back home, and he was making medical arrangements for our return. That was the deal, more or less. Russ has lots of money and that always helps grease the machine.

I was more than nervous, time ticked slowly, but Annie eventually responded adequately to the treatments and was declared well enough to travel home within two weeks. The French officials presented me with lots of discharge papers to sign and a large bill to pay.

It was just great to get Annie out of the hospital and a green light to go home. It was a long flight. I was anxious and jittery. Annie, on the other hand, slept throughout whole trip – start to finish. I wondered where we were going from here? Was this the right thing to do, and would I be able to help get Annie back to her old self, or at least some semblance thereof, or minimally healthy enough to be independent. Did I really know what I was doing?

Canadian customs clearance took a while, but went okay, and we were home. Russell was on the other side of the glass waving and waiting for our arrival, flowers in hand. "Hi, how was the flight? You look great Annie." Of course his eyes focused on her wrists and he grimaced.

She smiled, "Thanks, Russell, it is nice to see you, too." Hugs and kisses on the cheeks and then we were on our way. Russell loaded the luggage. Annie took the backseat, and I sat shotgun. Russell has always been so skillful at small talk that you almost get sucked in to thinking it was a real conversation. Nevertheless, I was thankful for his help. It was a relief to know that he was there. The ride was somewhat sombre, we arrived without much substantial speech exchanges, and began unloading luggage.

"I loaded your refrigerator and pantry with some essential supplies," Russell explained as he was dropping us off at the lower Dunbar Street townhouse. He has keys to water my plants and get the mail when I am away. I call him my agent. "Annie, I stocked you up with lots of those ramen egg noodles you love," Russ said while heaving the last suitcase to the curb.

"Thanks Russell," Annie said with another kiss on the cheek, "you are the best." She picked up a big bag and headed for the door.

That was it, we were definitely home, and it was the first day of the rest of our lives. Annie and I spoke about pedestrian pursuits, historical anecdotes, and then she said, "I'd like to go to bed and sleep for awhile now."

I scrambled around and set her up in the bedroom saying that I was not tired and planned on doing a little paper work. "I'm just going to crash on the couch when I get tired," and gestured towards the den. "You get some rest. I'm right here if you need me. It's going to be okay Annie, don't worry, we are going be just fine, trust me." And with a firm hug I left to let her sleep.

For fourteen hours Annie slept soundly. I went in and checked on her a half dozen times until she emerged, ate a bowl of cereal, and went back to bed. I really had no idea of what was ahead, and I was not all that confident, but we plundered along playing by ear, touch, and trepidation. We met with Dr. Quan and the UBC medical mood disorder clinic crew regularly. We tried a variety of new meds, monitored and measured their efficacy. One foot in front of the other and we stumbled forward on the road to recovery.

There were a bunch of low points along the way, and there was nothing linear about the recovery road. It was a two-steps forward, three back, stand still, and turn to the side for a while, but Annie was alive and that in and of itself counted for something. Mood swings were almost harder to deal with than the deep depression days where you could almost see a black cloud aura over her head. I learned to read the signals, signs and navigated accordingly. I had more patience in the beginning, got frustrated at times, and learned to cope and not sweat the small stuff. Medicalizing everything and medications had their place, but not a panacea.

My stepsister Ronnie's best friend, Lisa Fitzhenry has diabetes. She explained that insulin does not cure her diabetes, but without it she could not function. She would indeed die. Ronnie could tell when Lisa had missed or forgot to take her insulin. Once Lisa took the required dose, everything was okay. It was like clockwork. It worked well.

I understood the diabetes insulin medication compliance response process and tried to transpose it to Annie's condition without any success. Of course, Annie's mental health was completely different than Lisa's diabetes. Of course there was a biochemical imbalance in Annie's brain, but the meds were always an experimental trial, and when they worked it was sporadic and short-term. The threshold never stayed the same. At times it seemed like we were always playing chemical catch-up? Annie took one pill for this and then another capsule for that. It was like the old lady who swallowed a fly. Then she swallowed a spider to catch the fly, and then something to catch the previous intruder. It just kept going and going. Annie took blue pills for anxiety in the morning, but needed to take orange clonodines to help her sleep. Then she needed another regime to deal with lethargy. But, the mood swings cycled too soon. It was frustrating for everyone, especially Annie. The side effects were wicked, but I did not always know what was a side effect or weird behaviour. Well, that is, other than bloating, facial splotches, and tics. I could hardly remember the baseline, and the goalposts were always moving.

I tried explaining it to Russell, but he had never heard the song about the old lady before. "Are you serious," I asked, "I cannot believe you have never heard the song before? The old lady who swallowed a fly, you have not heard it?"

"Hey man, I didn't grow up in fairytale or near Disneyland, we bourgeoisie are a special breed. I learned stock market folk songs, Mozart, and cultural classics," Russell replied.

"The old woman who swallowed a fly is a classic," I cried! "You have heard it," I insisted. Alan Mills or Rose Bonne wrote it way back in the sixties or so.

"Yeah, how does it go, sing it for me, maybe the penny will drop?" he asked.

I cleared my throat and started out, "It goes like this:

There was an old lady who swallowed a fly.
I don't know why she swallowed that fly,
Perhaps she'll die.

The was an old lady who swallowed a spider,
That wiggled and jiggled and tickled inside her.
She swallowed the spider to catch the fly.
I don't know why she swallowed that fly,
Perhaps she'll die.

Russ was looking at me with a tilted head so I stopped. "Go on don't stop," he encouraged. "What happened next?"

There was an old lady who swallowed a bird.
How absurd, to swallow a bird!
She swallowed the bird to catch the spider
That wiggled and jiggled and tickled inside her.
She swallowed the spider to catch the fly.

I don't know why she swallowed that fly,
Perhaps she'll die.

There was an old lady who swallowed a cat.
Imagine that, she swallowed a cat.
She swallowed the cat to catch the bird,
She swallowed the bird to catch the spider
That wiggled and jiggled and tickled inside her.
She swallowed the spider to catch the fly,
I don't know why she swallowed that fly,
Perhaps she'll die.

I stopped for a second to check if he was still with me. "You following so far?" I asked.

"So far so good," Russ smiled.

There was an old lady who swallowed a dog.
She swallowed the dog to catch the cat,
She swallowed the cat to catch the bird,
She swallowed the bird to catch the spider,
That wiggled and jiggled and tickled inside her.
She swallowed the spider to catch the fly,
I don't know why she swallowed that fly,
Perhaps she'll die.

Russell now joined in singing the chorus,

There was an old lady who swallowed a cow.

I don't know how she swallowed a cow!

She swallowed the cow to catch the dog,

She swallowed the dog to catch the cat,

She swallowed the cat to catch the bird,

She swallowed the bird to catch the spider,

That wiggled jiggled and tickled insider her.

She swallowed the spider to catch the fly,

I don't know why she swallowed that fly,

Perhaps she'll die.

I finished the tune with a baritone voice:

I know an old lady, who swallowed a horse,

She is dead, of course."

"Wow, man," Russell whistled, "I did not know you were so talented. But, hey, you seriously think Annie will die?"

"I hope not," shaking my head, "so far so good, but I don't know. Paris was a while ago now. Everyday forward counts for something, eh?"

"Pete, are you still nervous about leaving her alone?" Russell asked. "You can go out, can't you?"

"Careful, I am cautious and careful," was my reply. "I want the glass to be half-full, but I'm realistic, too. Annie does not have diabetes or a positively directly treatable diagnosis; it is a mental combination biochemical and mind debilitating disease that evolves and morphs.

It just isn't that easy to get a differential diagnosis. The antipsychotic meds don't always work for everyone."

"Really," Russell exclaimed, "You told me it was schizophrenia?"

"It was, and it is, insidious schizophrenia" I replied, "but it is not that simple. And along the way it has morphed and became more complicated than the original label."

"You cannot get more complicated than insidious schizophrenia, can you?" Russell asked. "I couldn't do it," he sighed, "I think you are doing a saintly job Pete. I really do."

It wasn't about me; it was Annie. I was just a simple sideline coach. A cheerleader, a fan in the stands, "Yelling, you go girl, go."

Annie does the heavy lifting. She endured delusions, but she was convinced they were real. She endured the meds, but she was certain they were poison. We had huge fights over her compliance and whether the meds were working. Whenever I acquiesced over the meds she always took a nosedive and we rode the rollercoaster of emotions, mood swings, delusions, and hostile agitating behaviours that were hard to understand or tolerate.

Turned out some of the meds were actually poisonous. They were toxic, but we were rolling with the *experts'* advice and we trusted that they knew best. No medical malice, however, it was an ongoing experimental excursion to unknown destinations. It was tough. We waddled along wondering whether things would get better, or was this it, would we always live this way? I mean it was not always purgatory, but the days of sunshine, butterflies and blue skies were often overshadowed by too much gloom and doom. Too often the windows would not open wide enough for fresh air to fill the room.

Bob Dylan said, "*I was so much older then, I am younger than that now.*" I love Annie Jarman. Too many times when I go out to work or run errands I think I will come home and find her dead, but so far so good. I have no idea what I am doing daily and I have no idea of where this ship is heading, but the late great beautiful Beatle, George Harrison, wrote, "Little darling, here comes the sun."

VIII.

CRANIAL CHEMISTRY

Smoke slides under the door, you don't notice it at first, you can't see it coming in, and then it has suddenly filled the whole room. Smoke doesn't smash and bash the door down with a single blow. It happens so much slower. The next thing you did not know, because it happened below your level of consciousness, was getting overtaken with smoke inhalation. Then it is too late anyway, a done deal, what can you do, eh? At university I never really understood Freud's id, ego, and unconscious cognitive slips either, but who cares when it is just a theory. Real life, now that is a different matter altogether! Consciousness is not always quite what it is cracked up to be.

My Paris breakdown was a lot like smoke under the door. It did not happen all of a sudden, but gradually until it was too late and I was too far-gone to even know what was going on. Guess I was lucky in some ways, but not to the extent as the morons in my therapy group. They called their psychotic breakdown a "blessing." It was not a blessing by any stretch or imaginary hallucination, but I suppose it could have been worse. That is, of course, it would have been much worse without my old friend Peter Mackintosh. I would not have been released from Victor Hugo's Paris hospital if Peter had not arrived to advocate on my behalf. Mind you, I was so heavily medicated that I really do not remember all that much, but I had to get creative about the events because the mental health people will not accept the haze. It was all about the ABCs for them: Antecedents produce Behaviours that create Consequences. That is it. Once you can convince them that you have an understanding of the ABCs you will be okay. They won't let you go home if you cannot explain the ABCs. I know, it is stupid, but hey, it is the mental health industry we are talking about here. Moreover, the view is better from the outside, and at a distance, too. Monet's paintings are just like that; you have to stand back a bit before the image is in focus.

Peter was cool, calm, and always connected. I was in a Paris hospital without a lot of knowledge on how I got there, but I knew the sooner I got out, the better it would be in the short run, long run, and any other way of looking at the whole mess. I can remember the depression part, but I definitely do not remember taking a sharp serrated edged knife and sawing my wrists to shreds. I admit to making a few mistakes while waltzing through this dance of life, it happens.

The *final* suicide note was actually just one of many versions I had previously penned. They all had the same theme. It was getting to be anthologized. My shrink says, "Prior suicide ideation often serves as a precursor to premeditated suicide behaviours." I got a new shrink.

Dr. Charlotte Rossman helped me start the slow slide to the other side of depression, oppression, and self-understanding methods to cope with the mental mania of my maladaptive behaviours. At first we met twice a week at her Yaletown office to do biofeedback, Eye Movement Desensitization Reprocessing (EMDR) therapy, Jungian synchronicity imagery, but mostly we just talked. The talking therapy helped. Didn't feel the nausea or bloating as from the pills and my head got clearer.

Charlotte tried to get me to explain the "context" of my suicide attempt, "What were you thinking; what was going on in your head?"

I really tried to keep up my part of the therapeutic alliance. "You will get out of therapy what you are willing to put into it. It involves work and commitment."

Okay, but thinking about the context and what was going on at the time it was hard to answer. Sure, the suicide attempt was impulsive and stupid, but I was in a bad space. My pity party was a real rocker.

I guzzled a carafe of expensive French red wine, ate some Prozac pills, followed with a few old tiny Amitriptyline pills I had left in an old stash tin. The cocaine belonged to my ex-husband Michel. He had left it in a box in the basement labeled: junk. I did not imbibe it all at one time, but the timeframe was blurry anyway. Who knows where the hell Vicodin came from?

Guess I went all Whitney Houston and climbed into the bathtub. I really do not remember sawing up my wrists with the serrated chef's knife. So when they kept asking why I did that I really could not remember. So, I made up a couple different versions of why I did it.

The bathtub overflowed and I did not die. The neighbour downstairs had water dripping into his place from the ceiling. He complained and the building's superintendent used her master key to my apartment, discovered me in the tub, and that was that. I woke in the hospital some time later.

Again, as I may have mentioned, I have made more than a few mistakes along the way, but I'm trying to get it right. It is not easy.

IX.

SCHIZOPHRENIA'S RULE OF QUARTERS

Canada quit minting pennies on May 4, 2012. Since 1858 when Canada established its own currency the penny was circulated, but not any more, it's all over now.

Annie and I were waiting for our appointment with Dr. Quan. I was ruminating over whether I had put enough quarters in the parking meter. We had been coming to the UBC Centre For Brian Health regularly and I have picked up more than a few parking tickets. Annie could not care less about tickets, but I do. We rode our bikes a couple times, but I hate to be late for a meeting with Dr. Quan. Annie likes Dr. Quan, but she can't keep time worth a darn. Keeping time is my responsibility and consequently we drive the Jeep more than bike. Annie takes time to get ready to go out. I just grab a jacket. Good parking spots are hard to get.

I know Dr. Quan is important, but I don't think he sees many patients. There is never anyone else in the waiting room, but us, and no one ever comes out of his office leaving an appointment. Diana Franson, RN, is the nurse/receptionist. On a recent visit she also disclosed that she was also Dr. Quan's main research associate.

During our last appointment with Dr. Quan he explained psychiatry's *current* view of schizophrenia and the *Rule of Quarters*. Afterwards, I left with more questions than answers and Annie was again just happy to leave. She still worries that things will go sideways and she will end up back in the hospital. Of course, I constantly tell her to the contrary. "Over my dead body, or an Appeals Court order will you go back to the hospital. I've got you. You're staying at home. Worry about something else if you need to worry about something. The hospital is not worth the worry!"

Schizophrenia has a long history, most of it spurious and unkind. Same thing with autism, years ago they said it was something the mother did or did not do that caused autism. Psychiatrists called them *refrigerator mothers*. Really, they flew that flag way too long. Finally, some preeminent shrink said it was a mistake and they all turned and travelled a different direction. Picking on already suffering mums was pretty mean and too cruel to think true.

In 1899 Emil Kraepelin was one of the early scholars to write about schizophrenia. He called it premature dementia (dementia praecot). He was wrong and it took too long for the community to correct the construct. Dr. Quan explains that we need to understand that we can see psychosis, but the diagnosis does not have a blood test or x-ray to define and identify. Early detection is one thing and treatment is another.

Identifying and diagnosing Annie's condition has been quite an ordeal. We knew something was wrong. We just did not know what was wrong. Her confused thinking was one thing, while delusions were another issue altogether. Dr. Quan said, "I don't have a clinical crescent wrench for treating Ms. Jarman's symptoms."

So we did treatment via a trial and error process. Really, we experimented, and tried to find our way out of the woods. We tried one thing after another in an attempt to stabilize symptoms.

Dr. Quan's view of medication was analogous to shining a flashlight through a window. Too high and no light gets through. Too low and no light gets through. You hit the wall. We hit the wall a lot.

Basically, I understood the *Rule of Quarters.* Dr. Quan's explanation was that twenty-five percent of patients recover completely and go forward living without any problems. Twenty-five percent improve markedly few some relapse and they need some supports. Twenty-five percent need considerable supports and show a poor prognosis. The final twenty-five percent do not do well at all and ten percent of that group commit suicide.

At this point in time Dr. Quan's considered opinion was that Annie fell in between the first two quadrants. "Nevertheless, we must remain vigilant."

Sometimes we felt mentally drawn and quartered. The *Rule of Quarters.* Really, what a deal.

X.

WHICH WOLFE WAS IT?

My dad was erudite. I am not. Now don't misunderstand, I do not hold any self-actualization issues or self-esteem shortages. I am just not that erudite. And for the life of me I cannot remember whether it was Thomas Wolfe or Tom Wolfe who said, "You can never go home again." One of them said going home again was a bad bet. Which one was it?

Russell was late, I was early and that was par for the course. We were theoretically meeting around five in the afternoon at Jerry's Cove, the pub at Fourth and Alma Street. I got there at 4:30, and just after 5:30 Rusty strolled through the door like the Carly Simon song: You are so vain.

"Rusty, nice chapeau man," I said with a sincere complimentary smile.

"Oh yeah, here comes the Francais, eh," Russell replied with an intermediate intensity slug to my shoulder. "I bought this hat at Elsies on Granville Island. The same type of hat was more than three hundred after tax dollars at Rosens."

Russell was all about after tax dollars. He had recently served as a Senior Special Prosecutor on a high profile tax evasion case. Russell won a large settlement for the government. If one was not careful Russ would launch into a sermon on how paying taxes is the most important civic duty a citizen owes society.

"These guys want lots of government services, good roads, excellent medical care, parks, and schools, but yet they try and evade paying taxes! Bring down the hammer on 'em." Russell would say. "Do what you want with after tax dollars, but pay your share." Russell's rant was more than familiar to me. I had heard various versions many times before.

Russ is a belt and suspenders prosecutor. He covers all the bases and leaves nothing to chance. His legal trousers are secure.

The waitress came over to ask for Russell's beverage order, but timing is everything, "Nice hat," she said with a smile, "what can I get you."

Just to expedite the process, and not let Russ get started all over on the chapeau business, I jumped in with "He will have one of these," as I held up a pint of dark amber draught.

And with that the waitress pivoted and took off. Dogs can sense stranger danger. So too can an astute waitress. Maybe it is beta or theta waves. Maybe it is just a vibe. But no sense in dead end engaging when it does not matter the waitress should get in and get out. There was no need for to get involved with any in a protracted discussion with Russ. Zero sums no matter how you added it. Russ can be difficult that way.

"You going to order some food?" Russ asked.

"Naw, thought we would have a couple beers here and then head over to lower Dunbar. Annie's cooking dinner and she would love to see you."

"Yes, great, sounds good to me. How is Annie doing? Hope she's cooking curry. I love her curry."

With a big smile I was able to report, "Annie is doing well, really well. It's been over nine months since she came off all the meds. She is stable and doing well."

"Aw that's great news Pete, glad to hear it. You two have been through the wringer and back, eh. It's been a tough couple years since Paris?"

Nodding and smiling at his antics, I had to ask, "Russ, who wrote you can never go home again?"

Off the top of his head and without hesitation, "Thomas Wolfe," Russ replied, "and to be correct, the title is you can't go home again. Many people confuse Thomas Wolfe with the 1960s new journalism's white suited Electric Kool-Aid Acid Test Tom Wolfe. Both were great writers from completely different historical eras."

Taking a sip of the promptly delivered pale ale Russell continued by explaining, "The title, from the posthumous publication, you can't go home again, comes from the denouement of the novel where Wolfe's main character realizes nothing stays the same in an ever-changing world. And all those fond childhood memories of the past are not sustained if you try to return. Basically, in common parlance, it means once you have gained fame or acclaim you will fail if attempts to relive a distant youthful past are endeavoured. After you have played in the NHL your old peewee team will not take you back, even if you wanted to go back. So, Pete, this your way of telling me about moving back to Montreal?"

"No, not Montreal, but yes, we are moving."

"You can't go home again Pete, but I wouldn't go back to Paris, either."

"Cape Lazo, I inherited the old beach house where I lived as a kid. Annie and I have been back a few times and decided to move back permanently." I tried to explain the attractions of a rural lifestyle. The notion that the rural *quality* of life has more attractions than the urban *quantity* of life made little impact on him.

Russell smiled, and I garnered yet another shoulder slug, "Wow, what about work? You're too young to retire!"

"I'm not retiring completely. Greg Frenton is taking over the Gastown office and I will commute to town when necessary. Otherwise, I will work as a country lawyer, nothing to it. You could do it."

"Really," with a sincere scoff, "I don't think so!"

"Okay, ok, but you will visit," I insisted.

XI.

GENTLE GENETICS

Guess I had sat in the bathroom for quite a while. Don't know how long I was perched on the toilet looking at the second pregnancy test, but it had become dark outside and none of the inside lights were on when I eventually emerged. I stumbled around fumbling for a light switch. And just then Peter waltzes in through the front door.

"What's up Annie," he asked while switching on additional lights, "what are you doing in the dark?"

"Nothing," I blurted through a torrent of tears.

"Hey, hey, hey," Peter tried to placate something I knew he would never understand while reeling me in with a hard hug. "Its okay, c'mon, its okay."

"No Peter, it is not okay," I broke free and bellowed, "I am pregnant!" Sniffling, snorting, and spewing more tears, "I don't know how this happened. I mean I know how it happened I just didn't think it would happen. I just didn't think." And that was the truth, too. I had been over two years since Paris, over eight months since going cold turkey off all meds, and I mistakenly interpreted the biological defensive mechanism known as morning sickness as the more familiar feeling of nausea that had plagued me for so long from all those stupid medications. My biochemistry had been out of whack for so long that normal was not mine to know. Clearly, this was not a planned pregnancy.

"Is that the test stick," Peter asked?

"Yes," as I held it up, "the second test stick!"

"Okay, ok," he took it from me and gave it a shake.

"Peter, shaking the stick changes nothing, I am still pregnant!" I said a bit louder and shriller than was likely required given the situation.

He smiled, took a closer look, and said, "Wow, Annie, this is great news. We are going to have a baby."

He was happy, smiling, and acting all cool about the whole thing. I was completely freaked out. "What am I going to do?" I asked.

Changing facial expressions quickly, Peter calmly said, "We will do the right thing. Whatever you want, we will do the right thing, Annie." With another hug he softly said, "It's going to be okay. I love you Annie."

"I love you, too. But a baby, how will that work?"

Peter says I always catastrophize everything. Maybe I do, but he likes to think of himself as a glass half full man. Even though Peter preferred a bona fide medical diagnosis he agreed to go to the pharmacy to purchase a *third* stick. Of course, as soon as he left I surfed the net to see how accurate these pregnancy tests were touted.

Dating back to Hippocrates and ancient Greeks, pregnancy tests had a storied past of showing false positives and false negative. Not so much with modern methods, which simply detect urine markers with close to perfect accuracy.

The third test was positive. I knew it would be, but that OCD part of me is just another empty defensive coping mechanism. At age thirty-nine no one considers me a spring chicken, certainly not the medical community. And I had to agree as really I had no business bringing a baby into this planet, but there we were, and everyday it was happening full steam ahead.

Amniocentesis is a prenatal test designed to detect chromosomal abnormalities. I had two of them, one at fifteen weeks and the other at twenty weeks of pregnancy. Both were negative for Downs, Turners, Fragile X, and the fetal DNA was normal. It was a great relief, but my anxiety was still off the Richter scale. Genetically speaking I was good to go with a clear bill of health.

Peter was not the least bit anxious he was excited. We were registered for early bird prenatal classes. Peter called them pre-noodle classes. We could know the baby's gender from the amino test, however, we decided to wait and be surprised.

Peter is pronoid and I am paranoid, ying and yang. I did not want to start telling people about the pregnancy until I was farther along. The idea of a miscarriage plagued me just as much as the antithesis.

We had Russell over for dinner and broke the news. His reaction was as contained as could be without appearing negative. Russ plays a lot of poker. Of course, the next day when Peter was at the office Russell popped by to give me the third degree about how did I think this baby thing would work.

It was a good thing. We were both crying in the end, but it seemed like a good thing. And I had Russell's blessing – so to speak.

"I can't believe it Annie," Russell blurted, "You and Pete are having a baby!"

XII.

PENULTIMATE POSSIBILITIES AND A PUPPY

I have known Annie Jarman for a long, long time. Met Peter Mackintosh when we were at law school. They are the best friends I have ever known. When they asked me to stand up for them at their civil wedding ceremony I was honoured beyond belief. I was the best man.

For legal purposes in British Columbia a civil wedding ceremony must have two witnesses. Carin Barrington, Peter's high school friend from Cape Lazo served as the other witness. Peter cautioned me saying, "Whatever you do Russ, please do not refer to Carin as a *Maid* in Honour. The word maid might set her off. She is a feminist and can be touchy about language issues."

Of course, I said, "Whaaat!" with a sarcastic scoff. "She is the Maid of *Honour* and I emphasize the word honour!"

Turned out Peter was wrong, Carin is really quite cool, a little quirky, opinionated, but not that feministically sensitive about language. I liked her. And she is good looking, too.

Peter was correct about the title issue. It was a civil ceremony and he could not proffer me the best man title. I took it regardless, and churches notwithstanding, I was *the* best man. I enjoyed the honour.

After the City Hall civil ceremony the four of us went for a lovely dinner at Vikram's Kalongi Curry House on Arbutus Avenue. We all had a lot of fun. Annie and I enjoyed listening to Carin's stories about Peter as an adolescent stuntman bike rider and their sailing exploits. Peter admitted that at first he was reluctant to leave Montreal, moving sucks, but it turned out to be one of the best things to happen.

"I will always cherish those last days at Cape Lazo with my father," Peter said with a growing tear in his eye. "We had some quality time together. It was good. I still really miss him, everyday."

"Hey, hey, ho, Peter," I couldn't let him slide into a maudlin mood. "Before you dampen down the dinner with the blues, this might be a good time for me to give you and Annie the very best wedding gift of all time!"

I got up from the table and said, "Hold tight, I'll be right back." I had hired a dog person to meet me in the restaurant's parking lot. It had taken some maneuvering, phone calls, breeder forms and money, but I was able to secure a Newfoundland puppy from the Newfoundland region where Peter's dog, Bosun, had come from. For years I have heard Peter go on and on about his dog Bosun. I figured he was due for a new one. His dog Bosun died years ago from old age. It was time, great gift, eh? Everyone, except me, thought it was a dumb idea, but I didn't care. They were getting a puppy.

The parking lot was crowded; I looked around and heard a horn honk. It was my dog guy. I scurried over to the minivan, gave him more money, and we put the puppy into an aerated box with a ribbon on top of the lid. Jimmy, the dog guy, assured me that everything was copacetic. The puppy had been fed, watered, and pees all the time, "So don't worry about it."

Although the restaurant has rules about dogs, I had already paid off the manager so it would not be an issue. There is always an exception to the rule, eh.

Strolling into the restaurant with the box held tight I had them clear a spot on the table and made the grand presentation. I think it went over well.

Peter lifted the lid and wailed, "Russell, what have you done!" He was smiling and shaking his head saying, "You can't give us a dog!"

"Sorry, too late to tell me now," I replied.

Annie took him in her arms, "He is so cute!" She looked at me and said, "Thank you Russ, I love him! And I love you, too."

They now had a puppy and all the responsibilities that go with him.

XIII.

CAPE LAZO REDUX

Sitting here now, watching the waves wash over the sandbar in front of our rustic old beach house, with the rain tapping time on the bay windows and dormers; I can certainly retrace the whole thing and put it in context. I can reflect and recognize events as they had unfolded. Still, all in all, it is quite a saga.

After a lengthy illness Alan Maxwell passed away in the Montreal long-term care hospital facility where he had been living the past number of years. I visited frequently in the beginning, but the last few visits were not so good because of the dementia. He did not know who I was or what I wanted. Sometimes I do not know who I am either, but I felt so bad about Alan Maxwell's condition. I wished there was *something* I could do for him. He had really come through for me when I needed it. When my dad died, Alan Maxwell stepped up and helped me through a tough time. And I will always be indebted to him.

The long goodbye was so difficult and I was never able to reciprocate all he did for me. I think he knew how much I loved him. I hope so.

I had always been led to believe that the old Cape Lazo beach house that we had rented from the Johnston family was still under their title. However, such was not the case as Alan Maxwell bought the place some time ago. When he died his will revealed the Cape Lazo property was my inheritance.

Inheriting Cape Lazo was out of the blue and quite unexpected. But, in an odd metaphysical way I rationalized the stars alignment as a sign of some sorts. Annie was three months pregnant and the future seemed to be unfolding in unexpected turns.

The first couple sojourns back to Cape Lazo my mood was negative to poor. Things had changed. There were condominiums on the Point Holmes hill and spec houses littered the beach. A few strip malls and big box stores had sprung up along the main drag. A fast food place replaced my favourite pizza joint in the town. A lot of trees had been clear-cut. Dad hated clear cuts. A lot of trees were gone, and it took my breath away, the wrong way. It happens. Forestry is different in Norway.

Annie, on the other hand, seemed to show the same reaction I had the first time we set foot on Cape Lazo. Although over the years the old house had fallen in some level of disrepair, the bones and soul were solid. A bit of fixing up and it was fine. Carin Barrington's little brother Daniel was all grown up and an excellent carpenter. He got the house all ship-shape in short order - even with Annie's ever changing renovation and decorating plans. Carin had returned to the Comox Valley for who know how long, but she had agreed to serve as Daniel's assistant and/or apprentice to help repair our old house.

Annie was getting über pregnant. She claimed to be "nesting" and was obsessing over baby paraphernalia, clothes and accessories, but it was a healthy sort of obsessing. I was nervous. This was all quite new to me, and I was increasingly anxious, nervous, and reviewing all the prenatal notes, books, and sonograms. I did not really know what I was doing telling Annie that there would be no problems bringing a baby into the world. What was I thinking?

Too late now because on a sunny October day, Barbara Jarman Mackintosh was born at St. Joseph's Hospital in Comox. She was the most beautiful sight I had ever seen. Barbara J was perfect. Annie did it. Some screams, moans, and groans and then there she was out in the open world. I cut the umbilical cord and handed the baby to Annie. "Hello little one," Annie whispered so softly, "Welcome to our family!"

We spent the night at the hospital and returned home the next day. Russell and Carin Barrington had been busy with balloons and banners welcoming us home. Those two goofballs seemed to be clicking and connecting. Go figure, eh?

Three weeks later, Annie ever the agnostic invited everyone and anyone to Barbara J's "naming ceremony." In lieu of a christening the naming ceremony mushroomed into a really large event. Annie's brother Jedd was the Master of Ceremony. His partner, Serena, was a jewel, and looked after all sorts of arrangements that I would never ever have thought about.

All the Barringtons, including Carin, sat in the second row with Russell - who got all glassy eyed and tearful more than once. People who I had not seen in years had shown up to take part and bear witness to the naming of this new little girl. In the front row my stepsister, Ronnie gave me wink, and her new boyfriend, nodded with an approving gesture. My mum cried while Donald smiled ear to ear.

After the formal part of the naming ceremony completed, dinner was served and the celebration party got going full steam ahead. Toasts, speeches, and the assorted festivities were in order. It was the best of times. Smiles all way around.

I needed to take a short break and catch a breather from all the action. So I strolled down to the beach sat on the old cedar chair from way back when I was a kid growing up at the Cape. I thought about my dad, wished he were here for this day. Thought about Maxwell, Bosun, and Crazy Carin dancing up a storm with Russell.

Max, our new Newfoundland puppy had escaped from his enclosure and came tumbling towards me with little yips and yaps. Although he was way too excited with all the guests and commotion, he settled down quickly when I picked him up, set him on my lap and patted his fluff ball hair coat. "Calm down there lil' fella, things are going to be just fine. Max, my pup, you're going to love it here."

Cape Lazo Redux.

ACKNOWLEDGEMENTS

When I lived in Kye Bay the first few chapters of *Cape Lazo* were click-klacked out on my trusty Smith Corona typewriter (the same one that travelled to the Yukon and WSU).

Diana Quan Pengelley took the type written pages and transferred them to a floppy disc. I still have that disc in a desk drawer, but none of my current computers use floppy discs. Diana has always been helpful with text formatting and word technology. I remain indebted to her patience and skills.

Myra Crosley and Joanne Giampa helped with margins.

Professor Craig E. Jones, Q.C. explained legal scholarship monograph publishing in Canada. Although Craig bears no legal responsibility for any legal concepts in this book, he is always an inspiration and a prolific writer, too. My work is just fiction.

San Diego's Dave Dhillon gets credit for the epilogue to Part One. It was a good suggestion and helped the transition to Part Two.

The late great Marian Martin taught me many things. Everything I know about eagles was from Marian.

When Drew Carter was a student at North Island College in Campbell River I persuaded him to do some Research Assistant work on this book. We exchanged emails, phone calls, and got together when we could. Evidently, there was once a middle school called Cape Lazo. But, they closed it for cost savings. Although I have worked with a number of research assistants over the years, there is only one Drew. And he is the best.

While I have never flown from Comox to Vancouver, Kyle Carter has a large number of times. When he was ten he gave me the flavour of Chapter VII, Part One.

In addition to left-handedness, Enid Olive Julson Carter taught me how to drive a car and the art of storytelling.

Cody Leonard said, "You can't play video games all day."

Harbans says, "Just do what makes you happy."

JDC
Mayne Island
June 2012

2ND PRINTING ACKNOWLEDGEMENT NOTES:

Cape Lazo was first printed June 2012 at Oscar's Books on Broadway at Granville in Vancouver. Oscar's Manager, Barry Bechta and I designed the cover from a photograph I took on Mayne Island's Campbell Point. The book's body took a couple left-handed variations until we settled on a final version. We printed a hundred copies or so and I distributed them to friends and family.

Sadly, Oscar's Books is going out of business – such is the fate of many bookstores these days.

On a recent sojourn to Seattle I mentioned Oscar's demise to my long-term advisor R.S. Dinning. In *Cape Lazo* Ron appeared as a senior partner in the law firm Dinning, Maxwell and Meyers – hence, he has a bias. "What will happen to *Cape Lazo*?" Ron asked. I explained that although the original files are stored in the cloud, it is likely the death of the book because Oscar's won't be doing any more printing. "You can't have that," was Ron's reply. "That book is like one of your children. You have to keep it alive!"

Our friend Jeff Corigliano published *Terror Ridge* in 2012. Jeff liked *Cape Lazo* the story, but disliked the book's layout. "You have to go see my guy, Vladimir Verano at Third Place Press. He can fix your book."

Almost three years later Third Place Press and Vladimir Verano designed this version of *Cape Lazo.*

Vladimir Verano also designed my novel *Belle Islet Lady.*

Thanks Third Place Press for your continued support and excellent service.

Almost three years have passed since *Cape Lazo* was first printed. A few things have changed:

Cody Leonard now says you can play video games all day – if my mother will let me.

Kayden Carter says, "Be careful when you climb high, it hurts if you fall."

Harbans continues to say, "Just do what makes you happy."

ABOUT THE AUTHOR

JOHN CARTER is a licensed psychologist, Adjunct Professor at UBC, and a slow paddler off the Mayne Island Coast. In addition to academic and psychological reports he writes novels: *Crazy Cousins*, *Belle Islet Lady*, and *Cape Lazo*.

CPSIA information can be obtained
at www.ICGtesting.com
Printed in the USA
LVHW01s0357081117
555420LV00010B/73/P